Leslie Carlson is trying desperately to hold her family together.

With a sense of relief, Leslie let the story pour out. When she finished her pie, Dylan took her plate and wrapped his hands around hers, all without interrupting. She checked his eyes often for signs of boredom or rejection. Instead, gradually intensifying affection threatened to short-circuit her thoughts. "I never thought Vince would be so intolerant," she finished.

Dylan moved to let Granny sit on the footstool, but he retained his gentle grip on Leslie's hand. Granny clasped her other one. "I've no doot this is hard, luv. But ye cain't make yersel' responsible for your brithers' actions."

"But they're making life harder for Mum and each other."

"Sometimes we jist hae to let those we love feel their own pain. Tryin' to protect them enables them to continue avoidin' reality."

Leslie studied the hands clasping hers, one pair white and wrinkled, the other tanned and strong. Could she really distance herself from her brothers' struggles?

"Let me tell ye, luv, what I see." Granny smiled lovingly into Leslie's eyes. "I see a beautiful young woman who wants wi' all her hairrt to do what's right for her family. I see the same young woman becoming a prisoner within herself. Sometime I think Leslie Carlson is getting lost in the Carlson family.

JANELLE BURNHAM is from British Columbia, the setting for ***Midnight Music***, and has been writing for over ten years. ***Midnight Music*** marks her *Heartsong Presents* debut.

Midnight Music

Janelle Burnham

Heartsong Presents

ISBN 1-55748-448-1

MIDNIGHT MUSIC

PRINTED IN THE U.S.A.

one

Andrew's quick aim flung the basketball through its hoop to put his team three points ahead just a whisper before the buzzer indicated the end of the game. Leslie Carlson leaped to her feet with an ecstatic cheer for the Nipson BearCats' two-point win. Her "baby" brother had become one of the most proficient athletes on the Nipson Secondary School team, and only his coach watched him more intently than Leslie. But while Coach Williams watched Andrew's ball handling, she watched her "baby" brother's face. And now, while Coach smiled, she frowned.

Rather than grinning at the crowd as usual, Andrew simply shook his light brown hair away from his face and trotted to the bench. "What's with that kid?" Leslie muttered.

"Pardon me?" Her older brother, Vince gathered their coats and snack debris.

"Andrew."

He laughed and hugged her. "He played so well he made me look like a novice. Relax, Les. You worry too much."

Leslie grinned to make him think she believed him and looked up at the face almost identical to her own except dark brown hair topped his while deep auburn natural curls spilled over her shoulders. Both faces displayed hazel eyes, wide mouths, and large noses. Vince's height and rugged-looking features attracted admiration. Leslie felt her 68 inches and similar appearance made her look like a work horse—dependable, but not much for beauty. "My biggest worry is that if I ever have children one of them will have a nose like yours."

Vince twitched his shoulders indignantly, but his parents' approach blocked his protest. Both Dr. and Mrs. Carlson stood taller than average, though Mum's carefully styled reddish-brown hair and delicate features made her look fragile next to Dad's muscular 6'2". They were a good-looking couple, Leslie had decided long ago. Dad's friendliness perfectly complemented Mum's cultured grace. Though fifty-six years had added grey to Dad's dark hair, Leslie felt sure the humor in his eyes made him look at least a decade younger.

Now his brown eyes glowed with pride. "What about that brilliant ball technique we just observed?"

"I'm going to go talk with the hero." Leslie felt compelled to investigate Andrew's obvious lack of enthusiasm. A month ago, he would have grinned and shouted like a madman. This afternoon, he stood a little to one side, grim satisfaction etched in his guarded expression.

"Hiyah, buddy. Great game!" Leslie knew better than to hug him in front of his teammates, but had learned to communicate volumes in a handshake.

"Yeah. Not bad, I guess." He stuck his hand into her outstretched one, but without any answering pressure. She noticed how much he'd grown recently. He'd soon be taller than Vince.

"Why the dead fish?"

"Nothin'. Never mind, ok, Les? Tell the folks I'll be home later."

"But Mum planned—"

"She'll survive without me." He turned away, just

rudely enough to emphasize his desire to be alone.

Sub-zero air, typical of Nipson's northern winters, blasted Leslie when she exited the overheated gym and crunched across the snow to her waiting family. "Andrew's decided to come home later." She tried to sound nonchalant as she joined Vince in the back seat of their family sedan.

"Hmm, that's unusual," Dad commented. "He must be discovering independence."

Leslie hoped that identified Andrew's only motivation.

Seventeen years ago Daddy had placed in her lap a bundle wrapped in a fuzzy blue blanket. "This is your baby, Leslie. His name is Andrew. Mummy is still pretty sick, and she's going to need your help loving Andrew. Do you think you can do that?"

Loving him had been no problem. After her first glimpse of his tiny, wrinkled face, Leslie devoted every ounce of her little-girl affection to him. Daddy remained the most wonderful man in the whole wide world. She loved Mummy dearly, worshipped big brother Vince and big sister Karen, but Andrew owned her heart.

From the day Daddy brought him home until she tearfully left for school, Leslie filled her hours with Andrew's needs. Though she wanted desperately to learn to read, leaving him was the hardest thing she ever did. However, school had turned out to be lots of fun, and the day passed quickly. Even now, Leslie still felt the thrill that went through her as she returned home with Vince and Karen. They didn't notice, but she saw Baby Andrew standing at the window, their special watching-spot. She ran toward the house, and dashed in the door. He ran to meet her, screeching "Leelee!" She wrapped him in a hug so tight he whimpered.

Andrew started school five years later. Leslie walked him to his classroom each morning, and met him each afternoon for the walk home—best friends, confidantes, buddies. She listened to him read, practised his math facts with him and helped him with his homework as they got older. Mum bandaged his scraped knees, but Leslie comforted him.

Where had Andrew gone lately? Even when with the family, he acted far away—surly, short-tempered. His refusal to come home today illustrated just one of many such uncharacteristic moments. He almost always came straight home after his basketball games to share his triumphs and frustrations with his family.

Dr. Carlson parked in the garage. He walked around the car to his wife's side to open the car door for her. As always, Mum smiled tenderly at him as she got out.

Leslie loved to watch them. It represented to her why she had never been interested in more than friendship with any of the boys in high school. She couldn't define what she looked for. It had something to do with Dad's caring, his humor, mostly his selfless concern for his wife. If Leslie could find that selflessness even in seed form, she might be interested.

She tried to banish Andrew's problems from her mind while she visited with Vince. He'd made the six-hour trip home from university for Andrew's first hometown ball game in the secondary school championships and planned to return that evening. Though Leslie had outgrown her childhood hero-worship, she and Vince maintained a close friendship. They and their parents chattered incessantly through several games of checkers and an early supper.

She fell asleep still trying to figure out Andrew's changes, only to be awakened shortly after 2:00 a.m. by the banging of the front door. She threw her quilted blue robe around her shoulders, hurried down the stairs, and reached the bottom to meet Dad rounding the corner from his room. A staggering figure emerged from the shadows in front of the door.

"Whasha doin' up, Leshlie? Tolya I'd come home."

If she hadn't noticed the slurred speech, the reek of beer would have warned Leslie of her brother's condition. Pain engraved around his eyes, Dad reached for Andrew who staggered against the wall.

"No, no. Can walk m'shelf." Andrew tried to brush Dad's hand away. Instead, he half-fell, half-sat on the stair, leaned against the wall, and would have fallen asleep if Dad hadn't lifted him to his feet. Wordlessly, Leslie moved to Andrew's other side, helped Dad carry him to his room, lay him on the bed, and cover him with a quilt. Dad squeezed her shoulder in thanks and hurried back to his room before Mum awakened.

Leslie untied Andrew's shoes. Had this been his first drinking party? She couldn't help remembering the number of evenings recently that he had left the house right after supper and not returned until late. He always told them where he was going—to the library with the guys to research their science project, to Tom's house to help him with his algebra. Now Leslie wondered.

The uncertainty pained her more than his present condition. If this were his first drunk, the headache tomorrow would probably discourage repetition. But if he'd been lying about his whereabouts to get to these parties, he was obviously becoming dependent on something available there. A girl? Excitement? Alcohol? She smoothed his hair away from his face and took a last loving look at him. He was so typically teenage athlete, skinny and long-limbed. How typically teenager had he become in other ways?

Returning to her room too disturbed for sleep, Leslie wrapped herself in a handmade quilt which matched the blue and peach-colored decor of her room and curled up in the windowseat with a sense of brewing crisis. How would the rest of the family respond? She knew Dad would remain his steady self. Mum would most likely collapse into her private world. What would Vince say? He'd been studying for a psychology degree in preparation for a career working with troubled teens. Maybe he would be able to help. And her sister and brother-in-law, Karen and Brad? They had their own lives.

Leslie instinctively formed her thoughts into a prayer. "Father, I don't know if Andrew's trouble is as big as I think it is. I don't know what to expect, and I don't know how my family will respond. Will You show me how to cope so I can help them? And please satisfy whatever is missing in Andrew's life that is causing him to pursue. . . ."

Even before she finished, Leslie fell asleep, wrapped mummy-like in the quilt, stretched out on the window seat with her head against the window frame.

The shrill beeping of her alarm clock woke her a few hours later. She slowly sat up, trying to stretch the kinks out of her back and neck. Why hadn't she slept in bed? Gradually, the previous day's events returned to memory. She stumbled to her feet with a groan, then reproached herself. "Leslie Carlson, you handed that burden to your Heavenly Father last night. Let it go!"

Yet as she prepared breakfast for Dad and readied herself for church, she found it hard not to worry. She forced herself to rephrase her worried thoughts into positive prayers. The knot in her stomach gradually eased. By mid-morning, she could enter the church building with most of her customary anticipation.

Leslie loved Heritage Christian Assembly. She felt rejuvenated in the atmosphere of worship filling the buildings, and she enjoyed cheerful chatter with like-minded people.

Taking her seat in the choir, she deliberately turned her thoughts to the words of the opening hymn, "Living by Faith." She needed that reminder. By the time the pastor stepped to the pulpit for the sermon, she had forced her worries aside and felt ready to listen. He chose Psalm 91 for a text and used the reliability of God's protection as his theme. She nodded. The time had come for her to trust God to guard her brother, no matter what his problem.

Leslie had barely left the choir loft at the end of the service when a member of the College and Career group stopped her.

"Leslie, I just have to talk to you. I've heard the most incredible story, and I'm sure you'll want to know about it so you can put a stop to it."

"What's that, Maria?" Leslie tried to keep the alarm off her face.

"My brother James said he saw your brother Andrew in the mall parking lot last night in the middle of a beer party. I tried to tell him I was sure no one in your family would be so oblivious to their testimony, but you know how kids are." Leslie found Maria's shrill titter almost intolerable. "Even if the story were true, you know I wouldn't repeat it. Do we need to pray for your brother?"

Her gossipy tone cloaked in religious terms almost snapped Leslie's self-control. Leslie forced a smile. "I'm sure everyone in our church family would appreciate your prayers for one reason or another, Maria. Thank you for your concern." Without giving her a chance to reply, Leslie hurried outside.

Sunday dinner felt tense. Dad and Mum discussed the service and news from those in attendance. Leslie concentrated on keeping the serving dishes filled and on covertly studying Andrew. She didn't miss the way he pushed the meat and potatoes around his plate rather than eating, nor his preference for two cups of coffee instead of milk.

Leslie went to church alone in the evening. Andrew stayed in his room, where he'd retreated right after lunch; Mum had a migraine, and Dad kept Mum company. Leslie didn't feel like socializing, but the quiet tension in the house had stretched her nerves to maximum tolerance. She deliberately arrived a few minutes late and sat in the back row.

Pastor Quillan read from Nahum 1:3: "The Lord has His way in the whirlwind and the storm, and the clouds are the dust of His feet."

"What we see as clouds marring the blue skies of our lives are actually evidences of our Heavenly Father's Presence," he explained. "Even when those clouds become devastating storms, we trust our Lord to fulfill His purpose."

Leslie's tears flowed quietly. The sermon's perfect timing in the context of her circumstances resembled a cooling lotion on a nasty burn.

"Do ye need a hug, luv?"

Leslie looked up from her soggy tissues to find the service over and one of her favorite elderly friends standing beside her.

"Yes." She relaxed into the motherly embrace. Granny Maxwell had been a family friend since before Dad and Mum married. Widowed as a young woman, she had raised her three small sons single-handedly and well. Her boys now lived in various parts of the country, but Granny Maxwell chose to stay in Nipson, where she was "Granny" to many of the young people, especially the Bible School students.

"Shall we go home for a drap o' tea and a wee chat?" Granny asked.

"Sure." Leslie didn't feel like returning to her family just yet. Besides, a discussion with Granny would probably help.

Granny lived in an apartment in a senior citizens' complex adjacent to the church, so within minutes Leslie curled comfortably in one of her deep cushioned chairs. Granny bustled around making tea and cutting homemade granola squares.

"So, luv, what's troublin'?" Granny smiled sympathetically and put the tea tray on the coffee table between them.

Leslie related the weekend's events. When she stopped talking, Granny didn't try to fill the silence, but waited for whatever Leslie wanted to say next.

"I'm afraid, Granny," she whispered. She folded and refolded her tissue.

"Afraid of what, hon'?"

"Afraid that if I tell you what I'm afraid of, it will turn out to be true." Leslie grinned a tiny bit before biting on her upper lip to stop its trembling. "I think Andrew is drinking a lot more than we guess. Can teenagers become alcoholics?"

"Yes." Granny reached across the table to clasp Leslie's hand. "Why do ye think Andrew's troubled in that way?"

"Intuition, more than anything. He's changed a lot in the last couple of months. He's not the fun-loving kid I used to know. He's surly and spends a lot of time in his room alone or out with his friends. I haven't seen him drunk before, but I have a gut feeling this isn't the first time it's happened."

Granny waited a few minutes then said, "How aboot talkin' to the Heavenly Feyther?" Leslie nodded. Granny squeezed her hand and started praying quietly, her Scottish brogue thickening as she poured out her heart. "Our Feyther, I know you've given women, and especially mothers, intuition for a purpose. That gift and Your guidance helped me be mither and feyther both to my boys. Ye ken Andrew better than anyone, including Leslie who's been so much of a mither to him. His trouble's heavy on her heart, Abba Father, but we ken 'tisn't hers alone. Ye've allowed it tae come her way for a purpose that we may not understand until Heaven. Still we trust Ye, Feyther, and ask Ye to help us see your footprints in the dust aboot us. We ask Your peace as Ye show us Your face in this storm and thank Ye for it. Amen."

Occasional tears still escaped as Leslie drove home. Granny always defined the heart of a problem adeptly in prayer. Leslie no longer felt like an emotional pressure cooker, but knew she'd had a personal audience with God. Except for Andrew's bedroom light, darkness screened the house as she crept up the stairs. She tapped on his door, but he didn't answer.

two

Monday afternoon, Leslie gathered her geography notes off a small table in the student lounge of Nipson Bible School and stuffed them into her book bag. She'd been trying to study, but memories of Andrew banished her concentration.

"Leslie, have you noticed today's paper?"

She shook her head, hefted the strap of her well-stocked book bag onto her right shoulder, and turned toward the voice.

"It has an excellent picture of your brother at the game on Saturday, along with a great write-up. 'Nipson's Newest Star Leads Team to Last-Minute Victory.'"

The reader sat at another of the small study tables with the local newspaper spread in front of him. Leslie remembered Dad's eagerness to introduce this person to her just before Christmas. She still couldn't figure out why it had been so important. Dylan appeared older than most of the Bible School crowd, probably just past thirty. Leslie noted how his forest green sweater emphasized his thick, dark hair. Deep-set eyes, a square jaw, and broad shoulders gave him a rugged appearance softened by a ready smile.

"No, I hadn't seen it. I take it the article is favorable?" She settled the cumbersome bag on a nearby chair, hoping he wouldn't misinterpret her courtesy as flirting.

"Favorable's not the half of it." His green eyes glowed enthusiastically. "I'd say your brother is fast becoming a small-town hero."

"It's tradition." Leslie pretended sisterly boredom. "My older brother Vince did it, too."

"And you?"

"Nope. I'm as co-ordinated as a cow on marbles. Do they have any more of those for sale at the concession?" Leslie nodded at the paper.

"Go ahead and take this one. I'm finished and—" A sudden crash interrupted Dylan. Papers, pens, and books poured out of the fallen bag.

Leslie jumped to catch the avalanche, but tripped over an uneven pile of books. She tried to reach in eight directions to catch renegade papers. Her shin landed heavily on the edge of one of the thicker books. Her elbow slammed into a chair leg. Books and papers continued sliding and she wanted to cry from pain. However, her already wounded ego refused to submit to further humiliation. She struggled to find a more dignified and less painful position.

"See what I mean about a cow on marbles?" She tried to grin and smoothed her skirt over her knees.

"You didn't have to do that just for me." The amusement dancing in Dylan's eyes marred his sympathetic expression. He pushed back his chair and reached to help her with a large, angular hand. "May I help, or dare I get too close?"

"I think it's safe for the moment." Leslie scrambled to her feet, then gasped and stumbled when she tried to walk on the injured leg.

"Are you all right?" Dylan steadied her.

She settled gingerly onto a chair. "Yeah, I guess I just landed wrong." A mental picture of how she must have looked caused her face to burn.

"Is there a right way to land in this mess?" He evaluated the disaster around them. "Did all of this really come out of that bag?"

Leslie couldn't help giggling at his expression. "My dad says the only other thing in the universe the same size and density as my bag is a black hole." To her surprise, Dylan chuckled and started stacking books. Without thinking, she added, "Not many people understand my dad's humor. I use that line every time someone makes a crack about my bag, but most people just smile vacantly and change the subject."

Dylan laughed again. "I like it. I'm in your dad's theology and homiletics classes. Do you think I could get extra credit on my term project by giving you and all your stuff a ride home?"

"He would probably award you the Purple Heart for bravery." Leslie couldn't decide what to say next. The bag once again contained her books, and Dylan busily picked up the last few pieces of paper. "I didn't mean for you to clean up my mess."

"My privilege. You want to stop by the infirmary to get something for that leg?"

Leslie looked down at her still-throbbing shin. Several wide scrapes bled slightly, and the area had begun to swell. "Nah, I'm tough. I guess I'd better accept your offer of a ride, if you don't mind. Dad left at noon so I'm on foot."

Dylan's eyebrows pulled together. "Mind? I wouldn't have offered otherwise. Besides, I'd be a fool to miss a chance for extra credit." He folded the newspaper and tucked it inside her bag. Picking up the bag with one hand, he offered Leslie the other arm. "I think you'll need something to lean on."

Leslie felt awkward. She did need his arm for support, but he was practically a stranger. Besides, she didn't lean well. At least those muscular-looking shoulders weren't just for show. She could feel the hardness of his arm muscles beneath his sweater. This definitely wasn't a scholar's build. Leslie wondered what kind of work he did. His face showed evidence of many hours spent outdoors. To her relief, they reached the car before her brain could make any more uncharacteristic observations.

"Meet the Princess, Leslie." Dylan gestured as widely as he could with the book bag weighting his shoulder.

Leslie giggled again in spite of herself. Princess? The last name she would have thought of in connection with this large, yellow automobile. "How many city blocks does it take you to turn it . . . I mean, her around?"

"Three." Dylan grinned, deposited the book bag behind the passenger's seat and turned to help Leslie. She couldn't help thinking while he closed her door and walked around to the driver's side how nice it was to be treated like a lady.

Dylan turned the key in the ignition. Nothing happened. He jiggled the gear shift, twisted the steering wheel a bit, jiggled the gear shift a bit more and tried again. With a bit of a cough, the engine started. "I call her the Princess after the fairy tale about the Princess and the pea. Unless everything is just right, this gem doesn't run. Of course, my bank account's not overflowing, so I've learned how to hold my mouth just right to make her work. At least it gives her personality."

Leslie chuckled appreciatively. Guys who didn't idolize their cars were uncommon.

"You'll have to tell me where we're going," Dylan

reminded her.

"Oh, right. I'm so used to riding with other people, I just assume everyone knows where to go. You'll want to turn left at these lights."

"Thanks for the advance warning. Too many people give directions like, 'Oh, you should have turned back there.'" He glanced her direction with his infectious grin.

"Turn left at the next stop sign, right at the next corner, and we're the third house on the right. You see, I do live close enough to have walked," Leslie explained.

Dylan opened the door for her and reached in for the troublesome bag. "Not on that leg. Quit apologizing for doing me a favor. I've always wanted to see where my favorite professor lives."

Dad rose from the porch swing where he had been sitting with Mum. "Well, Dylan, this is a pleasant surprise. Honey, meet one of my senior students, Dylan Stoddard. Dylan, my wife, Joanne. I take it you've rescued my packrat daughter from her book bag?"

Dylan shook Dad's hand then greeted Mum. "Pleased to meet you, Mrs. Carlson. Leslie had a bit of a mishap, so I offered her a ride. She told me Dr. Carlson might consider giving me extra credit for my term project based on exemplary service."

Mum just smiled, but Dad had his answer ready. "Anyone brave enough to take on my daughter's book bag deserves some kind of reward. How about supper?"

"May I take a rain check? I have this homiletics exam Wednesday. Unless, of course, you discuss your tests over dinner."

"I refuse to let Dad talk about his classes at the table." Leslie glanced mischievously at Dad, then turned her attention back to their guest. "How about Wednesday night to recover from your labors?"

"It's a plan." Dylan nodded to the three of them and turned to go. "By the way, Leslie, an ice pack will do wonders on that leg. See ya' later."

"Leg? What did you do, dear?" Mum's eyes looked red and strained.

"Nothing, Mum. It's just a little scraped and swollen."

"He's such a nice young man. Why haven't you said anything about him before?"

Leslie took a deep breath for patience. She looked at Dad, whose eyes betrayed his amusement. He enjoyed these mother-daughter discussions about the men, or lack thereof, in Leslie's life.

"He's not even in my class, Mum, and he's obviously quite a bit older."

"That shouldn't be a problem. Your dad is eight years older than I am."

"This is the first time I've said more than hello to the guy. Is Andrew home yet?"

Mum buried her face in her hands and Dad shook his head. Leslie noticed for the first time the weary lines around his eyes and mouth. "He came home around 2:00. What's for supper?"

Leslie knew the signals. Something was badly wrong and Dad had spent the afternoon putting Mum back together. He would talk to Leslie later, but not in front of Mum. She did some quick thinking. What would Mum probably enjoy most for supper?

"Spaghetti sound all right to you, Mum? I can thaw out some sauce I froze last week and put together a salad quickly. If you want to make garlic bread, I bought French bread yesterday."

It took Mum a couple of moments to respond. "That sounds good, Les. Do we have enough soft butter?"

The distraction seemed to be working. "I think so. Let me get changed and I'll meet you in the kitchen in about twenty. Okay?"

Mum nodded while Dad gestured toward the bag Dylan had left beside the door. "I'd offer to help with that, but not being a body builder I'm afraid I'd strain something." Leslie decided not to honor the gibe with a reply. Limping up the stairs, she noticed Andrew's closed door. She set the book bag inside her bedroom and went back to Andrew's. "Hey, buddy? It's me—Les. What's up?"

"I just want to be alone for awhile." His voice sounded muffled. Was he lying face down on his bed? "Can I eat up here tonight?"

"Let me check with Dad." When one of them was having a crisis, family custom permitted that person to have one meal in the bedroom, subject to Dad's approval. "Sure you don't want to talk about it?"

"Maybe later."

At least he'd made his request politely—an improvement over his previous sullenness. But home at 2:00? He obviously wasn't sick, so something serious must have happened at school. Leslie knew better than to try to second-guess the crisis. Mum needed distraction right now. Hopefully kitchen togetherness would help.

Mum stayed quiet at the supper table and only ate minimal servings at Dad's gentle insistence. Leslie sympathized. Emotional distress always destroyed her appetite. However, if Mum skipped meals every time she felt upset . . . Leslie refused to finish the thought. Mum needed loving attention, not criticism.

She put a hand on Mum's shoulder when she returned from carrying leftovers to the kitchen. "Don't worry about the dishes, Mum. Would a hot bath with some of my lavender-scented bubble bath help you relax?"

"That sounds good, dear. Thanks for the delicious meal. I'm sorry I wasn't hungrier."

"Don't fret about it. Your garlic bread was a treat."

Obviously concerned, Dad watched Mum slowly make her way down the hall to their room. "Thanks, Les. You really did help this evening." He hugged her. "How about if I take Andrew's meal up to him while you clean up? He can do his own dishes later."

"Sure, Dad. Meet in your study in about ten minutes?"

"Give me half an hour. I want to make sure Jo is settled." His small smile faded quickly.

Leslie found him reading Psalms when she brought him hot mocha. His eyes looked brighter. "You know, some days I think the Psalmist must have looked into the future and over my shoulder while he wrote." He smiled his thanks as he reached for the cup.

"Or maybe it's a case of rough days being timeless. Isn't that comforting?" Leslie leaned back in the recliner, setting her hot chocolate on a nearby end table.

"Our Father's love and control is also timeless, something I'm prone to forget. Les, Andrew got a week's suspension from the basketball team today."

"Suspended? Why?"

"Drinking. It's a team rule—anyone who gets caught with an alcoholic beverage gets suspended. Coach Williams actually went easy on Andrew because this is his first offense, but he acted far from pleased. I guess he saw

Andrew shortly before Andrew came home Saturday night."

"Uh-oh. How did Andrew respond?" Leslie pushed the recliner back up to a sitting position and moved to the front edge. Her hands trembled.

"He was furious when he came home, but he's cooled down enough to realize he asked for a lot worse than he got."

"It's not like him to be so obnoxious."

Dad smiled sympathetically at her frustration. "Leslie, every parent asks questions about every child at one time or another. You've all had your definition-defying days."

"But this is more than a day or two." She sighed. "He hasn't been himself since Christmas."

"I know." Dad shrugged. "I don't know why for sure, though I'm beginning to suspect. You have your own suspicions, don't you?"

"Yeah, but saying it out loud makes it seem more threatening. You think it's alcohol?"

Dad nodded. "If we're right, Andrew's not the first teenager to be trapped. It will take a lot of discreet watching, as well as prayer."

"Has Mum noticed?"

"I don't know." Dad swirled the last bit of liquid in the bottom of his cup. "She's moodier than usual, so she may be aware of more than she's admitting."

A question rose to Leslie's mind, but she hesitated. Dad never scolded her for making an honest inquiry; neither had he allowed any of his children to play him and his wife against each other. "Dad . . ." she paused.

His eyes looked up from the cup he had been studying, though his head didn't move. They communicated a love and respect that reassured Leslie.

"Does Mum have some sort of problem? I've known she wasn't a typical homemaker, but I figured that was just Mum. Lately, her reactions have made me think there may be more to it."

"I know what you're asking. In fact, I've expected it and tried rehearsing tidy explanations." Dad sighed deeply after a few moments of silence. "I haven't found one that works. I guess I should start with a preamble. I don't believe in family secrets. Besides that, I trust you too much to be anything less than honest. That means saying some difficult things about Joanne. Please remember I love her even more today than I did the day we married."

Leslie nodded understanding.

"It started before Andrew's birth. She experienced a difficult pregnancy and delivery. In fact, I almost lost her. Thank God I didn't." He rubbed a hand across his eyes as if to erase the memory. "She remained bedridden for a couple of months after he came."

Leslie remembered those days as exciting. Granny Mesler had come for a long visit, and then Nana and Papa Carlson. She had never thought about how serious Mum's illness had been, or how worried Dad felt. She waited for him to continue.

"After those first months, it became obvious that your Mum had lost emotional, as well as physical, strength and that it would be a long time before she would be able to handle the normal demands of a home and family." Dad smiled affectionately. "Until you took over, housekeepers kept the clothes washed and meals on the table. As you kids have grown, Jo handled a little more, though her emotional weakness is her refuge from anything she doesn't want to face."

"What about Vince and Karen? Have they realized her problem?"

Dad sighed again. "No. Karen never had any trouble too big to be solved by a quiet talk with Mum, and teenage boys tend to take their mothers for granted. Brad Ferguson filled up Karen's life after high school, and Vince went straight from high school to university. Neither of them is as analytical as you." He grinned to let Leslie know he was not criticizing.

"Can Dr. Marshall give Mum antidepressants or something?"

Dad carefully centered his cup on the coaster before answering. "Jo has retreated so far into herself she's unaware anything is wrong. Both Dr. Marshall and I have tried to talk with her, but we can't get through. Her world consists of what she wants to acknowledge. That's why any kind of crisis brings on hysteria. It forces her to face something uncomfortable."

"But it's been almost seventeen years. How have you coped?" Compassion filled Leslie.

"I won't pretend. The first couple of years were downright miserable. I felt cheated, confused, and frustrated." Dad ran his fingers along the edge of his Bible, lost in thought as he remembered. "Finally, my misery forced me to take the problem to my Heavenly Father and stay silent long enough for Him to talk to me. He reminded me that when I married Jo, I promised to love her as myself. People say love is blind. It isn't. Love just chooses its focus. Many of my wife's fine qualities are not obscured by her illness, not the least of which is her love for me. She adores me like many men of my acquaintance wish their wives would adore them."

"You called it an illness, Dad. Is that really what it is?"

Dad looked straight at Leslie. "Yes. Many well-intentioned people have told me that if she just decided to get well, all our troubles would be over. I wish it were that easy. Maybe she will recover some day and maybe she won't. That's immaterial. I have chosen to love her until death separates us, and love her I do."

His words replayed in her mind like a cassette tape while she straightened the house for the night and prepared for bed. She couldn't help wondering again how Mum would respond if Andrew's problems turned out to be serious. That, of course, would make life even more difficult for Dad. Maybe Andrew's suspension would startle the kid back to being himself. If not, there had to be a way she could untangle his struggle before it became a disaster.

three

A kaleidoscope of unrelated thoughts tumbled through Leslie's mind during the ten-minute ride to school with Dad on Tuesday. Andrew's reluctance to go to school this morning bordered on defiance. First he pleaded illness, then stomped and banged around in spite of Mum's migraine. Tomorrow night's supper needed to be planned. A nagging feeling about an upcoming quiz hovered at the edge of the confusion, but Leslie couldn't remember which class had scheduled it. She'd had neither the time nor the inclination to open her books last night. If a quiz appeared on today's agenda, she'd just have to wing it.

Dad always arrived at school an hour before classes began, so Leslie flopped her bag on a table in a corner of the student lounge. Yesterday's newspaper with its headline announcing Andrew's success caught her gaze. The four-column photo had been a clever shot, catching Andrew in the spring just before his concluding basket. The expressions on the faces of his opponents said it all.

A shadow fell across the table and a voice inquired, "Mind if I sit with you?"

Leslie kept her gaze on the page while she formulated a reply. James Trindle. She didn't have to look at his face to visualize his self-satisfied expression. She knew his eyes studied her from behind round tortoiseshell framed glasses. He used his height to intimidate, while carefully cultivating the perception of a polished, scholarly appearance. Leslie thought his tweed jackets with suede elbow patches looked dated rather than erudite. She felt his attempts at charm made him appear even more plastic than his usual snobbishness. Her instincts warned her not to prolong the encounter. Yet, she didn't want to be rude. She forced a small laugh. Even to her ears it sounded more like a snort. "Why not?"

James seated himself beside her. Leslie hoped her cringe didn't show. She had attempted on several occasions to convince him that the seat across from her would be more convenient for conversation. She heard him draw in a deep breath and prepared herself for a speech.

"Miss Carlson, I've made no secret of my regard for you. I trust you will believe what I am about to say is prompted by that regard and nothing more. May I continue?"

Leslie only nodded, unable to think of a polite way to halt his pomposity.

"I noticed the article you are reading. I have been acquainted with your family for some time, so I consider your brother almost part of my family. Of course, as Christians, we are all part of God's family—which means I have a responsibility to both you and Andrew."

Leslie wanted to shout, "Get to the point!" but knew she could only wait until James's self-importance led them there. She braced herself for the inevitable.

"I believe my sister expressed our concern to you on Sunday about where I saw your brother Saturday evening." James didn't even wait for her acknowledgment. "She felt you might have been offended by her approach, which I freely admit is not always as tactful as it might be. I apologize on her behalf and for not anticipating that the difficult news might better be communicated by myself, since you know I have nothing but your best interests at heart. This unfortunate front-page trumpeting of Andrew's success compounds my concern. Such adulation can only be harmful for one as young and impressionable as your brother, who has already demonstrated his inability to maintain a Christian witness in all situations."

Leslie waited for the onslaught to continue, but mercifully, James seemed to have finished. How should she reply? She couldn't give him the respectful appreciation he expected. She studied her watch and stood. "Mr. Trindle, I'm not even going to thank you. We're proud of Andrew and glad to see him get the recognition his athletic skills have earned for him. Now, if you'll excuse me, I have a class to attend."

She folded the newspaper quickly and left the lounge. How many more times would she have to put up with James before he realized she did not feel attracted to his inflated ego? She quickly turned right to enter her geography classroom, colliding with a slender, grey-haired man who had to tilt his head upward to look her in the eyes. At the same moment, she remembered which professor had announced a quiz for today.

"Oh, I'm sorry, Dr. Jonas! Did I hurt you?" She dropped her bag and reached to steady him. "I wasn't watching where I was going, and I apologize. I don't know what happened to my mind." She could feel a bright blush working its way from chin to forehead.

"I'm not made of cut glass, my dear. You didn't even shake me up." Dr. Jonas gestured toward the doorway. "After you, ma'am. If you weren't Leslie Carlson, I would guess you had spent too long saying good morning to some young man." He followed her into the classroom and settled at his desk purposefully. His bushy grey mustache twitched, which meant he found his own comment highly amusing. Sixty minutes later, she gathered her books, determined never to be unprepared again.

Leslie spent the next class period devising a number of schedules and checklists on which she could rely. She knew a rigid study schedule wouldn't work. The unexpected, like last night's chat with Dad, always happened. But a checklist might work—just a simple list of upcoming assignments, quizzes and exams with their due dates. By the time Child Development class dismissed, Leslie felt confident her list included everything important.

"Uh, Leslie, may I . . . uh, speak with you for a moment?" Dylan's voice caught her attention just outside the classroom. He stood uncertainly to one side of the flow of students through the hall, as if trying to blend his muscular frame into his surroundings.

"More than a moment if you like, Dylan. My next class isn't until 11:15."

Dylan didn't respond. With a protective hand on her elbow, he steered her into the study hall toward a deserted table. He handed Leslie a folded up newspaper. "Your dad stopped me on my way out of homiletics and asked me to give this to you."

Leslie unfolded the most recent issue of the daily. "You must have snatched this off the pile when the delivery arrived this morning. Are you sure the print isn't still wet?" She laughed and looked up.

His somber expression didn't change. Instead, his green eyes reflected the pain that roughened his voice. "I don't know how your dad found it, but please, just read the front page. We can talk later."

She unfolded the paper fully and bit her lip as she read the bottom headline. "'Nipson Secondary Hero Suspended for Drinking.' That didn't take long."

"You're not shocked?" The shadows in his eyes lightened, though his gaze never wavered from her face.

"No, we discussed it thoroughly last night. At least Dad and I did. Andrew isn't communicating with us right now. Maria and James are going to love this."

"I'm sorry."

Leslie studied the article surrounding a reprint of Friday's jump shot picture. At least the facts hadn't been garbled—yet. "I take it Dad has read this?"

"Yes. He told me where to find you."

"How did he react?"

"Mostly concerned about you. I would guess he's been through similar crises."

Leslie remembered Dad's tone when discussing "well-meaning people" last night. "Perhaps, but I think this is his first with one of his children." Her mind raced with various methods of squelching gossip before it reached Dad. The only truly effective way would involve being everywhere at once.

"Leslie." Dylan interrupted her thoughts with a disconcertingly gentle voice. "Please don't fret about your dad. You'll wear yourself out if you try to protect him. He's a strong man." Raw pain showed on his face.

Dylan's accurate perception of Leslie's thoughts unnerved her. She suddenly felt vulnerable, not a common or pleasant sensation. She stood and jammed the paper into her bag. "Thanks for your concern. However, this is *my* family. We're familiar with difficulties. Thanks for helping Dad get this to me. I have to run to class." She squared her shoulders, gave him a brief smile, and left the room.

For all her attempted independence, Leslie's mind whirled helplessly. She knew she had been rude. She also knew Dylan just wanted to help. Why should he care? He couldn't understand her position, so why try? Yet his apology indicated he wasn't trying to meddle.

She arrived at her next class just in time to find a seat. Good. She didn't feel like chitchat. She forced herself to concentrate by taking unusually detailed notes. Maybe she could join Dad for lunch.

Leslie barely waited for the professor's dismissal before heading for the door. The halls were extraordinarily crowded. She pushed her way through the swarm, for once heedless of whom she shoved out of her way. She saw Dad just leaving his room. "Hi, Dad. Want to join me for lunch?"

"I'd love to, but I have staff meeting. Did Dylan find you?" He locked the door while his keen brown eyes searched her face.

She turned to accompany him down the hall, easily keeping pace with his long-legged stride. "Thanks for the paper."

"I didn't want you to find out secondhand. Sorry I don't have time to chat." He stopped beside the staff room doorway. "By the way, I'm leaving early. Dylan will give you a ride home again."

Exasperation sharpened her voice. "Dad! I can walk."

"I know you can, but I thought you might appreciate the break. See you later."

Leslie felt tears gathering. She'd been counting on a talk with Dad to help her regain perspective. Not only did he not have time to talk, he seemed unaware they were headed for a storm of major proportions as soon as the rest of the world read the paper. Then to send her home with Dylan!

Leslie dreaded that ride all afternoon. To her dismay, Dylan greeted her in the hall immediately after her last class and reached for her bag.

"May I help with your time bomb?"

She didn't want to be rude again, so she relinquished the burden. "Thanks. I'm sorry you got commandeered into playing taxi again."

"Don't worry about it. I offered."

Leslie didn't say anything more, but walked out quickly ahead of him. Concentrating on her own scrambled thoughts, she didn't notice the glaze of ice created by an afternoon warm wind, called a "Chinook" by Northerners. She stepped off the last step onto the parking lot and felt her feet slide. Arms suddenly steadied her from behind until she regained her footing.

"Oops! Thanks, Dylan. I always take one major tumble every winter. I figured this was it. Thanks to your great reflexes, I guess I have a reprieve." Dylan made no effort to respond. Didn't he know his kindness made her feel even more unsettled? She continued babbling until she felt ridiculous. Her words ran out when they reached the Princess.

Dylan just looked at her and let the silence linger. When he spoke, he sounded gently serious. "Um, Leslie, I'm sorry I offended you this morning. I truly didn't mean to meddle and I shouldn't have said anything. Will you forgive me, please?"

Surprise snapped Leslie's gaze away from the snow-covered pavement to Dylan's face. His eyes reflected sincere concern. Leslie wished she could laugh the question off with a witty reply, but Dylan's seriousness deserved the respect of absolute honesty.

She shifted her concentration to his shoes. "I forgive you. It just seems everybody in the world knows how to solve my problems, and I haven't figured out what's happening."

Dylan just nodded and reached behind her to open the car door. Leslie settled herself in the seat, and blinked hard. By the time Dylan buckled himself in the driver's seat, she had lost the battle.

Silently, he fumbled in his pocket and handed her a sparkling white, carefully folded handkerchief. "It's been in my pocket only twenty minutes," he said comfortingly. A trace of humor lingered around his eyes, but his face mostly communicated understanding and caring.

Leslie's tears didn't stop until the car turned the last corner before the Carlson house. She felt foolish for her emotional reaction, yet incredibly safe. As though it didn't matter that she'd fallen apart. As though Dylan understood. She didn't know what to say so she folded the handkerchief and stared at her lap.

"Looks like you have guests." Dylan brought the car to a stop at the curb.

"Oh, great!" Leslie gasped at the four-wheel drive, multilighted, two-tone half-ton pickup parked in the driveway. "I forgot, and they're already here!"

"Forgot what? Shall I keep driving?" Dylan smiled mischievously.

"No, but thanks for the offer. That's my sister and brother-in-law here for my nephew's six-month birthday party. Would you like to come in and meet them?"

"Are you sure? I can't stay long."

Leslie nodded. "It won't be all that formal, just an excuse for the family to get together."

Dylan hurried around to open the door for her. "Does it mean I can't come tomorrow?"

Leslie grinned and shook her head. "No, that's your reward for survival."

"I don't think survival will be a problem. Your dad's tests are tough, but relatively easy to study for. Besides, a year of Dr. Jonas's geography quizzes prepared me. The man only calls them quizzes so he can announce them the day before."

"Don't I know it!" She sighed. "I completely forgot about one he announced last class. It was close, although it's kind of hard to mess up 25 points worth of multiple choice. I don't know where my mind went yesterday—forgetting the quiz and tonight's party. I spent class time after geography designing a checklist for schoolwork so this won't happen again. Looks like I may have to add domestic items."

"You need me to call you the evening before your quizzes and exams to remind you?" Dylan's smile contained a hint of teasing.

"The idea has merit. Watch out, we've been discovered."

The front door burst open and a large, huskily built man strode out onto the porch to envelope Leslie in a bear hug. "And how's my favorite sister-in-law?"

Leslie wrapped one arm around him, wondering why Brad always boomed rather than spoke. His sandy-colored hair looked like he hadn't combed it in a week and his blue eyes sparkled with fun and affection.

He released her quickly to extend a hand of greeting to Dylan. "Pleased to meet you. I'm Brad Ferguson."

"Dylan Stoddard."

"I hope you'll be joining the party." Brad led the way into the house. "Hey, honey, come meet Leslie's guy."

Leslie wanted to crawl under the carpet. She had half-expected this kind of reaction, yet hoped to avoid it. Karen appeared in the doorway of the entry, her face alight with interest. "Hi, Leslie. I didn't know you had a boyfriend."

"I don't. This is a friend of mine from school, Dylan Stoddard. Dylan, my sister, Karen."

Next to Brad, Karen's 5'4" blonde, blue-eyed slenderness became diminutive. Leslie had often been tempted to envy her sister's fragile-appearing femininity, but with characteristic common sense realized it was wasted effort. Envy would not reduce her height, or change her solid bone structure. Besides, she had a party to plan on the spur of the moment.

She hurried into the kitchen, exchanging a brief greeting with her parents in the living room. Mum had claimed Li'l Brad, Karen's six-month-old son. She and Dad were playing pat-a-cake and peekaboo with him. At least Mum's headache had apparently abated. Leslie heard Brad and Karen leading Dylan into the living room, then Dad's delighted greeting.

Leslie quickly set out fresh vegetables, chips, and dips on a portable table and rolled it into the large, sunny living room. Mum and Karen were discussing baby food, diaper rash, and grocery prices. Dad and Mum still shared the baby on the couch, and Brad and Karen snuggled on the loveseat. Leslie watched them while she filled snack plates, and smiled to herself. Karen had been fortunate to find an openly adoring husband like Brad. He could be loud and brash, but he obviously loved Karen and their baby wholeheartedly.

"Hey, Les, these cracker things are pretty good. Guess we won't need the help of the walking vacuum to clean them up after all," Brad teased. "By the way, where is he?"

"The condition of your plate doesn't leave you much room to twit Andrew about his food consumption," Leslie returned. "Is this thirds or fourths?" She glanced at Dylan, perched on the piano bench beside the loveseat. "Is Brad leaving enough for you?"

"Of course not. I'm dorm-fed, remember?" Everyone laughed at Dylan's attempted pathetic expression.

Leslie's mind skipped from thought to thought, refusing to stay focused on a single subject. Andrew's problems, Dylan's observations, Brad and Karen's probable reactions to Andrew's problems, the way Dylan fit so comfortably with their family, Dad's attitude toward the article, Andrew's change in attitude. . . .

Engrossed in her mental treadmill, she didn't notice Dad until he put his hands on her shoulders from behind. "What's the worry?"

"Worry?" she tried to laugh. "Who's worried?"

"You always sing in the kitchen unless you're worried about something. Is it Andrew?" He turned Leslie to face him.

She met his gaze, searching for reassurance.

"Leslie, you're assuming too much responsibility." His voice was kind, though his words were sharp. He tipped her chin up so she had to look at him, and smiled just a little. "I've already shown Mum the article. Remember our agreement to let our Heavenly Father guide us through the problems?"

"Yeah, it's just easier to fret. I always feel like I have to get things figured out." She reached up to squeeze Dad's hands, then turned back to the stove before the potatoes boiled over. While draining and mashing them, Leslie forced herself to release emotionally each of the problems.

By the time she served supper, everyone sounded in rollicking good humor. The guys swapped jokes and ridiculous stories, keeping the women speechless with laughter. But Leslie noticed Mum's eyes looked strained. She suspected Mum wouldn't have participated in the gathering had it not been for Li'l Brad. Dad gave her extra-solicitous attention, making sure Mum's water glass remained filled and that the serving dishes sat within easy reach. Li'l Brad provided entertainment by playing peek-a-boo around Karen's attempts to feed him, then smearing mashed potatoes and gravy all over his face and the high chair.

Good-naturedly groaning from over-indulgence, the men moved from the table to sprawl in various locations in the living room. Mum and Karen took Li'l Brad to the bathroom for a change of clothing. At another time, Leslie might have resented being left with the dishes; tonight she felt grateful for the solitude. She hummed quietly as she cleared the table.

"May I help, Cinderella?"

Leslie jumped at the sound of Dylan's voice. Water splashing into the sink had muffled his approach. "If you want, unless you had planned to leave right away. I've handled dishes for this crowd on my own before."

"I'm in no hurry to leave. Besides, I'm hoping you'll talk to me while we work." Dylan rolled up his sleeves and plunged his hands into the soapy wash water.

"Talk about what?"

"Anything you want. Dr. Jonas's latest jokes would do or what you like to do with your spare time."

"Spare time—what's that?" Leslie dried and put away the dishes he had washed. "I hear people talking about it, but I can't seem to find a supply of it for myself."

"Unexpected parties don't help, do they?"

Leslie blushed a little. "This has been on the agenda for months. The excitement of the last week just drove it out of my mind." She picked up a stack of clean dry plates to put in the cupboard on the other side of the kitchen. Dylan quickly dried his hands and reached around her to open the cupboard door. Leslie looked at him in surprise. "How did you know it was that one?"

"I watched you set the table."

The thought that he had been observing her so closely left Leslie speechless. They silently finished the dishes while a myriad of adjectives for him whirled through her mind—unbelievable, gentle, perceptive, enigmatic. She watched him drain the sinks, rinse the stoppers and carefully fold the dishcloth over the oven door handle. Yet, she couldn't bring herself to say more than, "Thanks for helping."

"My pleasure. Sorry I have to run, but my homiletics teacher's almost as tough as your geography teacher." Dylan smiled apologetically.

She heard him make his farewells to the group in the living room. The front door clicked shut behind him, and she wondered why she suddenly felt lonely.

four

"Smells like you got the best of Murphy today, Daughter," Dad teased when the aroma of moose roast greeted them upon arrival home Wednesday afternoon.

"I won't count on it until supper dishes have been washed and put away," Leslie replied. "I still have the mashed turnips, corn-on-the-cob, spinach salad and apple pie that may or may not go wrong between now and supper time."

"Sure you don't want help?"

"That's a sure way to put Murphy's Law into effect." Leslie laughed at Dad's pretended hurt expression. "You can help most by staying out of the way until your guest arrives, then keeping him out of my way until I call everyone to the table."

"Stay out of the way she says. How's that for filial piety?" Dad inquired of the walls. He patted Leslie's back, then hurried to his room to check on Mum.

Leslie ran up the stairs, pulling off her sweater on the way. Dylan would be here in two hours—plenty of time for preparing the meal, but Leslie's nerves demanded the release of frantic activity. She stared at her open closet. She needed clothing that wouldn't be ruined by a kitchen mishap, but she didn't want to look like a rag bag. Her tan cords would look nice with her green sweater, but did she want to risk staining them?

Maybe her newest pair of jeans would work, not too

fancy, but still attractive. Would her green sweater be too warm in the kitchen? Probably, but—she stopped in mid-thought. Why was she so worried? Dylan was Dad's guest and would probably spend the evening with him. What did it matter what she wore? Besides, she couldn't afford to waste time.

She quickly pulled on a pair of green socks, then her jeans. She grabbed a yellow blouse from the rack, and topped it with her green sweater. It seemed important to don a pair of large earrings which matched both shades in her blouse and sweater. A fluffy cloth barrette pulled her hair away from her face, which she inspected quickly for make-up flaws. "Stop it, Leslie," she told herself with irritation. "You're the cook tonight, not his date!"

Supper preparations continued flawlessly. She sang while she peeled and chopped turnips and assembled the apple pie. She always kept pie crust dough in the refrigerator to cut down on preparation time on evenings like this. Did Dylan like apple pie? Most men did.

She examined the royal blue table cloth critically. Did it have too many wrinkles? Probably not, since the peach placemats would cover most of it. Vince often teased her about using both a tablecloth and place mats, but Leslie liked the effect. Though Andrew hadn't been home for supper in almost a week, Leslie set a place for him anyway. Peach and blue flowered china and blue-toned glasses completed the table setting. She folded the last napkin in a hat-type pattern and heard Dad greeting Dylan at the door.

Better check the meat. Moose overcooked easily, but this roast looked perfect. Leslie grinned to herself. "Beat you again, Murphy." With the meat out, the pie could go in the oven. The mashed turnips sat invitingly on the back of the stove to keep warm and the corn looked about done. She had to make sure she remembered croutons and dressing for the salad.

"How's Cinderella tonight?"

Leslie started and looked over her shoulder. Dylan's grinning face peered around the corner. "Don't harass the cook," she teased. "It could be bad for your health."

"Anything I can do to help?"

"You can lift the corn out onto that platter beside the stove."

Dylan moved confidently to the stove and followed her instructions like a pro. The front door slammed again. To Leslie's amazement, she heard Andrew's voice in the entry.

"Am I too late for supper, Leelee?" He only called her that when he felt in an affectionately good mood.

She carried the meat fork with her to greet him in the hall. "Not a bit, if you hurry. Glad you're here, pal!"

"Yeah. Got to missing your culinary skills." He grinned in his own lopsided way and disappeared into the half bath beside the entry.

Dylan had found the butter dish that matched the china and filled it from the supply in the refrigerator. "Want the juice and the salad to go out now, too?" he inquired.

Leslie suppressed her surprise at his thoughtfulness. "The juice can go to the table, but please put the salad on the counter next to the sink. I'm not quite finished with it." She smiled her thanks.

He carried the juice out, then filled each glass with ice. "I hope everyone likes ice in their beverages."

She reassured him and handed him the meat and turnips

to put on the table. "Thanks for your help, though visiting with Dad probably would have been more fun."

"No problem at all. He said he had to go check on your Mum, so I thought I'd make myself useful."

"That turkey. What a way to treat his guest."

"Actually, I feel privileged. Not too many women will let a man wander around in their kitchen."

"If that was wandering, I'd like to see you perform." Leslie noticed his face turn lightly pink, but his eyes told her he felt pleased by her praise. "Would you please call the others?"

She grabbed the salad and the dressing on her way to survey the table for last minute additions. Thanks to Dylan's help, everything looked perfect. Andrew flopped in his usual place at the end of the table.

Dad came in with Mum and seated her to the left of the other end. "Andrew, would you mind moving here next to Mum so our guest can have that chair?"

A dark scowl suddenly appeared on Andrew's face, though he slouched to the designated seat. Leslie looked at Dylan hoping he wouldn't be disconcerted by Andrew's rudeness. Dylan smiled reassuringly and moved to pull out her chair. "May I?"

The gesture surprised and delighted her even while she noticed Dad smiling smugly. "Why, thank you." She hadn't had someone help her be seated since the last family Manners Night years ago.

Dad said his customary short blessing over the meal. While the food passed from person to person, Dylan tried to draw Andrew out of his pout. After three monosyllabic answers, Dad interrupted with a deceptively mild voice. "Andrew, you know the rules. If you can't be pleasant at the table, you are invited to leave."

Andrew knocked his chair over backwards and stomped out of the room. Leslie heard his bedroom door slam.

"I'm sorry about the scene." Though he addressed Dylan, Dad looked at Leslie.

"Don't worry, Dr. Carlson. I know how obstreperous teens can be." Dylan directed his reassuring smile toward Leslie. "At the risk of making a pig of myself, may I have more of that delicious roast? It isn't beef, is it?"

"It's moose. A couple of the deacons like to hunt, so they give us whatever meat they can't use." Leslie passed him more roast and turnips.

"You don't like to hunt, Dr. Carlson?"

"Not really. No specific reason other than I'd rather have my fire in a fireplace where I can enjoy it from my easy chair."

"Somehow I had the impression that all of Nipson's male population adhered to the semi-annual hunt." Dylan's expression communicated curiosity rather than reproach.

"Most do. I'm just an odd duck."

"Now, dear, you're just fine the way you are." Mum spoke for the first time since the meal began. "How long have you been in Nipson, Dylan?" She tucked her napkin under the edge of her empty plate.

"This is my third year. I've fallen in love with the town."

"We quite enjoy it," Mum agreed. "What did you do before you came here?"

"I spent a few years on oil rigs in northern Alberta. My first job here in British Columbia happened about five years ago. That's how I found Nipson Bible College—the driller on that job attends Heritage Christian Assembly and invited me to go with him the weekend the job ended.

The rest is history, as they say."

"What did you do on the rigs?" Mum inquired.

"I was just a rig hand, a roughneck is what they called me."

That explained his muscles, Leslie thought, surprising herself. Though she knew little about the oil patch, she knew rig work ranked with the roughest and most demanding occupations.

"Is it dangerous?" Mum leaned forward with unusual interest. Everyone had finished eating, so Leslie began clearing dishes away.

"Loggers have more accidents," he explained patiently. "Though we don't have much margin for error."

"Do you still do that kind of work?" Leslie asked the question this time.

"It keeps me out of trouble during summer breaks." He smiled mischievously. "And gives me a useful appetite for real food."

"You want to reserve a little space for whatever she's concocted for dessert," Dad warned. "You can be sure it will be tasty."

"In that case, let me help clear the table so we can get to dessert sooner." Dad and Leslie laughed, and even Mum seemed amused by Dylan's childlike eagerness.

Pie and ice cream disappeared as quickly as Leslie served it, with Dad and Dylan indulging in seconds. Dad finally pushed his plate away and patted his stomach. "Mighty good eating, Les." He looked at Mum, who still picked at her pie. "Jo, shall we go start a fire in the fireplace while these energetic youngsters clean up?"

Mum didn't answer right away, but slowly pushed her pie away and stood up. Dad gently led her into the living room. Leslie carried the ice cream back to the freezer and began packaging leftovers. Dylan worked around her easily, moving back and forth from the dining room to the sink. Leslie looked up from stacking containers in the refrigerator to find the table bare except for the tablecloth and placemats.

"You're quick! Thanks." She turned to smile at him, only to find him at the sink.

He squirted a bit of dishwashing soap into the hot water before he returned her smile. "For a meal like that, I'll do just about anything."

"I'm glad you enjoyed it. I'm also sorry Dad keeps running out on you. You don't have to stay and help, you know."

"I don't mind this at all. I enjoy the opportunity to become acquainted with Dr. Carlson's family."

Leslie felt a twinge of disappointment that he said "family" rather than "daughter", but pushed it away. He and Dad had been friends for ages. Why should he see her as someone special? Besides, they had only actually met two days ago. She grabbed a towel for drying, but found Dylan had used rinse water so hot the dishes air-dried in seconds.

"Did you want me to wash this or is it just for decoration?" He flourished a green box Leslie recognized immediately as being the unopened croutons.

"Rats. Looks like Murphy got me after all. Those were meant for the salad." She put the box back in the cupboard.

"Which was delicious as served. Who's Murphy?"

"You're familiar with Murphy's Law—you know, 'Whatever can go wrong will go wrong'? Dad has gotten into the habit of referring to Murphy as though he were another member of the family and I've picked it up. Haven't you heard him mention trying to outrun Murphy?"

"Yes, but I just thought it was a dog or something. You never know with your dad." Dylan laughed and used a fork to lift the stopper out of the sink used for rinsing. "This hot water is great for dishes but hard on the hands. Got to watch it with these soft scholarly paws of mine."

Leslie chuckled. "Roughnecking doesn't sound to me like it would produce soft, scholarly paws."

"No, but the phrase sounds good." Again he carefully hung the dishcloth to dry.

"I'm curious. Where did you learn your way around a kitchen so well?"

"Partly Mom and partly living on my own. Practice will do it to you. Anything else to do?"

"No. You've earned your supper. How about taking a break in the living room."

Dad and Mum sat quietly on the couch, holding hands as they watched the fire. "I see your slave driver let you loose, Dylan. Hope she didn't work you too hard."

Dylan settled comfortably on the piano bench. "Not at all. I even got the bonus of meeting Murphy."

"Murphy? So he got you after all, Les?"

"Just the croutons, which should have been on the salad. Never mind. You didn't keep your part of the deal—as in entertainment and staying out of the way."

"Wh-what?" Dad's face looked cherubically innocent except for the mischief in his eyes. "Dylan, before my daughter maligns my character any further, how about some music?"

"I've heard Leslie's pretty good on the guitar. I will if she will."

His fingers danced easily on the piano keys in the introduction to a familiar Jewish-style chorus. She picked up her guitar from the corner behind the piano and joined in. Mum started clapping, and then Dad's rich baritone filled in the words. Before long, all four of them found harmony parts. Mum's alto blended beautifully with Dad. Leslie found a middle-soprano line, then heard Dylan fill in the bass harmony. She almost stopped singing in surprise. His speaking voice betrayed little of the rich bass notes he could sing. He moved easily from chorus to chorus, then into hymns, keeping them singing for almost an hour. He continued playing the piano, creating melodies and harmonies of his own. Leslie put her guitar down.

He raised an eyebrow. "Tired?"

"Just the fingers. Carry on. We haven't heard playing like that since Vince left."

Leslie let her mind wander with the music. Somehow it made her think of Psalm 23. She could hear the Shepherd's gentle voice and the trust of the sheep. A run of notes in the high range made her think of the still waters. Dylan moved into a minor key, bringing to mind the Valley, then a triumphant succession of chords which brought to mind the closing verse of the Psalm. "I shall dwell in the house of the Lord forever." Another full-chorded run ended the piece. Everyone remained silent for several minutes.

"Thanks for the incredible music," Dad finally said quietly. "Made me think of Psalm 23."

"That's what I call it," Dylan answered. "It sort of came to me one day when I was meditating on the Psalm and now comes off my fingers instinctively when I'm in worship."

"I'd like you to read that for us, if you will, Dylan, and

then Isaiah 40." Dad handed him a worn Bible from the coffee table.

He read well, Leslie noted, not pontifically as many read Scripture, but with expression as though wringing each drop of meaning from the words for the benefit of his listeners. "The Lord is my Shepherd, I shall not want . . . He tends his flock like a shepherd: He gathers the lambs in his arms . . . they will soar on wings like eagles; they will run and not grow weary, they will walk and not be faint." (NIV) He closed the Bible with a caress.

"Let's pray." Again, Dad made his suggestion quietly. To her delight, he seemed as deeply affected by the music and reading as she had been. She didn't know why that delighted her, but the reason didn't seem important. Brevity emphasized the depth of meaning in what they had heard.

"Well, Dylan, I don't want you to feel unwelcome, but my wife and I have to get off to sleep. Feel free to stay and visit with Leslie as long as you like, or as long as she lets you," Dad said with a teasing smile. "See you tomorrow."

Dylan sat silently on the piano bench for several long moments, gently running his fingers over the Bible he still held. Finally he looked at Leslie. "I don't want to seem ungracious, but conversation seems inappropriate after this last hour. Will you be offended if I leave right away?"

"Not at all. I would offer you some more pie or something, but I know what you mean."

She closed the door behind him and turned off the porch light. Suddenly she became aware that she hadn't thought about Andrew since he left the table.

five

Piles of clean laundry littered the living room floor. Three loads done, one to go. Leslie's Thursday classes finished by 2:00, which enabled her to go home early and catch up on housekeeping chores. No matter how quickly she started laundry after coming home, the job lasted well into the evening. Of course, she had been interrupted by Dad's request for an early supper before his 6:00 church board meeting. At least folding and sorting were mindless jobs, allowing her thoughts to follow other subjects. Lately, only two held her attention—Andrew and Dylan.

Picking up an armload of clothes for delivery to various bedrooms, Leslie remembered last evening with a smile. Though Mum usually avoided visitors other than family, she seemed to enjoy Dylan. But then Dylan's easygoing personality made him easy to like. Leslie still felt awed by the memory of last night's atmosphere after they finished singing. She tried to analyze why it made such an impression on her. Worship obviously motivated Dylan's music, which he played with the skill of a professional.

The telephone rang sharply. She threw a pile of Dad's shirts on top of the to-be-ironed basket and ran to answer before the noise disturbed Mum's nap.

"Good evening, Leslie, this is your sister."

Oh, brother, what had upset Karen now?

She didn't give Leslie an opportunity to respond. "We just picked up our mail this afternoon and I'm amazed no one saw fit to prepare us for the shock of Andrew's misbehavior. I do hope Dad read him the riot act. I'd also like to know why you wanted to keep this from us."

Leslie gripped the receiver so firmly her knuckles turned white as she tried to word her explanation carefully. "We didn't want to spoil Li'l Brad's birthday party. Besides, Dylan was there. You don't air family laundry in front of guests."

Karen replied sharply. "I don't blame you for not wanting your boyfriend to know about your brother. But I am your sister."

"Ok, Karen, I'm sorry we offended you and Brad. Give him my apologies. Now can we forget the subject?"

"Of course we forgive you." Karen's voice reverted to sweet femininity. "Just tell me one thing and I'll hang up. Dad *is* being firm, isn't he? We can't let Andrew think this is insignificant."

Leslie's head felt like it would explode from the building pressure of holding herself together. "I honestly don't know what Dad said to him."

"Well, I'm sure he'll realize the only solution is firmness. We can sure praise the Lord for using this little problem to bring us closer to Him, can't we? Li'l Brad's waiting for his supper, so I'd better run. Give my love to the parents. Bye."

Leslie replaced the telephone receiver with shaking fingers. Speaking of riot acts! She couldn't remember ever being so angry with anyone, especially a family member. Of course they hadn't mentioned Andrew's suspension during the party. Karen's sense of offense had mushroomed all out of proportion to the slight, not to mention her determination that Andrew be thoroughly punished like a recalcitrant puppy.

The phone rang again. Leslie barely restrained herself from snapping. "Hello?"

"Hi, it's the starving dormie." Dylan sounded so cheerfully mischievous Leslie couldn't help but laugh.

"That's better. When you first answered I thought I might get an earful."

"I tried to answer pleasantly." Leslie vaguely wondered why hearing his voice should so quickly soothe her lacerated feelings.

"You did pretty well, but I could still feel your brain waves."

Leslie laughed again. Dylan's upbeat goofiness was just what she needed. "They're mellowing out. What's up?"

"First of all, I wanted to thank last night's cook for a superb meal. It sustained me through one more day of dorm food."

"Is someone fishing for another invitation?"

"What a genius of an idea!"

"I'm pretty good at catching hints," she said dryly, trying to mask her pleasure at his enthusiasm. "Now that you've accomplished your first objective, what's next?"

"Tonight seems to be a perfect night for a walk in the snow. Care to join me?"

Leslie looked out the window in the front door at fat, thickly falling snowflakes. It could be fun.

"How about if I come over so we can discuss it?" he suggested cheerfully.

"Sure. I suppose you'll expect tea and oatmeal cake?"

"Like I said, you're a genius. See you in a flash."

Leslie continued staring out the window with her hand still on the telephone. She felt strangely reassured and delighted that Dylan wanted to come, but vaguely alarmed. Nothing said she couldn't be friends with the guy, but what if she became too attached?

"Leslie, you think too much," she scolded herself. "Just enjoy the evening."

The front door opened. Andrew slouched in and kicked it shut with his foot.

"Been awhile since I've seen you, buddy. How're ya doin'?" Leslie tried to keep her voice cheerful in spite of his dishevelled appearance and sullen expression.

"Leave me alone."

"Andrew, what is wrong?" Suddenly Leslie's control snapped. "You're treating us all like we have the plague. If we're lucky you say good morning to us when you get up but we don't see you again until the next morning. And last night you were rotten. How do you think we feel, lying awake at night waiting to hear the front door close so we know you're home safely?" She couldn't help the final sob that broke off her words. The sound echoed between them until Andrew spoke.

"Who has really missed me? How do you think I feel knowing the whole town is talking about my family because I was stupid enough to get caught with booze on my breath one night? What else was I supposed to do while the rest of the team celebrated?" His voice became high-pitched and nasal. "'Hey guys, I'm the golden-haired boy so I can't drink that nasty stuff. Coach might get mad.'" His voice returned to its usual tone. "I'm sorry I can't be what you guys expect." He stumbled up the stairs.

Leslie heard the kick that shut his bedroom door. She leaned against the wall and buried her face in her hands. Her best efforts weren't putting her world back together.

"Leslie?" The voice was hardly more than a whisper.

She looked up. Dylan stood just inside the door.

"I followed Andrew up the sidewalk. I didn't mean to eavesdrop, but the door didn't shut all the way." He shrugged apologetically and held out his arms. "Would a hug help?"

Leslie buried her face in his shoulder. She needed to lean on someone, anyone—just for a few minutes. Dylan held in her in a tight hug until her sobs quieted. With one hand he searched his pockets and pushed a handkerchief into her hand.

Leslie laughed shakily through her tears. "I still haven't washed and returned the other one."

"Don't worry. I have lots." His soothing voice wrapped itself around her. She felt his hand stroke her hair just once before he gently pushed her away so he could look at her face. "A walk in the snow might still be a good idea. The cake can wait."

She nodded, relieved that he had suggested action. With the storm of emotion passing, his embrace unnerved her.

He opened the entry closet door, retrieved her coat, and held it for her. "Want to talk about it?" he asked, closing the front door behind them.

She shuffled through the snow on the walkway, not sure what to say. "I don't know. Emotional overload, I guess."

"Family struggles can be life's biggest challenges," he agreed. "But you're handling it well, kid. Sorry—did I say something wrong?"

She forced a watery smile. "No. Just don't be nice to me until I get myself under control."

He nodded understandingly, squeezing her shoulders in a brief hug. "Any place special you'd like to go?"

Leslie watched fluffy snowflakes continuing to blanket the ground. She suddenly wanted to surround herself with trees rather than buildings. "Do you mind walking through the park behind the administration building? As if we didn't spend enough time on Bible School grounds."

Another smile lit his eyes. "Not at all. I discovered the park soon after I came to Nipson, and it's become one of my favorite places to wander." They paused for a street light to change and Dylan stuck out his elbow. "Would you like to hold on to me while we cross? These streets are still pretty slick." His smile teased her gently.

She slipped her mittened hand through the crook of his elbow. "Thanks. Where did you pick up your gallantry? Manners like yours don't show up often here in the North."

"I know. I grew up in Bayfield. Even though it's a metropolitan area, it still acts like a northern oil town."

"Vince has mentioned that Nipson's hick-town residents seem to have more class than our big city neighbors."

"My gentle little mother drilled into both of us boys that manners are no more than treating others with respect." His gloved hand covered hers on his arm.

"She's short?"

He laughed. "According to her, no. According to Dad and us boys, yes. She's about your height, but all of us are well over six feet, so we tease her a lot."

"I can imagine," Leslie said dryly. "Tell me about your family." Her hand remained on his arm, though they now wandered along park paths where the snow hadn't packed well enough to become slippery. He didn't seem to mind, and she found the physical contact comforting.

Dylan smiled affectionately, talking almost absent-mindedly. His dad served with the Bayfield detachment of the Royal Canadian Mounted Police. His mother happily devoted her time to homemaking. His younger brother worked as a computer programmer with a petroleum company.

"What about you? Unless I'm embarrassingly wrong, you're quite a bit older than the average Bible School student." She saw the teasing light in his eyes before she finished her question.

"That's because I was born several years before most of you," he explained sagely.

"Thanks. What took you so long to join our humble ranks?"

His expression sobered. They walked several moments in silence before he answered. "Let's just say it took me awhile to realize that my humanity needn't bar me from full-time church ministry."

Leslie let the subject drop. She sensed more behind Dylan's answer, but didn't feel like an in-depth discussion of anything tonight.

"Getting cold?"

"No. I'm just mentally and emotionally numb. Sorry for being such inspiring company."

Dylan stopped and looked directly into her face. "Leslie, please don't apologize for being human. I chose to be with you tonight, even after I knew it wouldn't be hilariously entertaining. I just want you to be comfortable enough with me that you can be yourself, whatever that happens to be at the time." He paused until she looked at him again. "You haven't had many friends, have you? I mean, kindred spirit types."

Leslie tried to chuckle. "I thought that only happened in books. Besides, with five hundred people in the school, why have you suddenly decided to be friends with me?"

"Would you believe it's because I like your dad's sense of humor?"

"Right."

"Then say it's because you didn't criticize my car."

"Sure."

"Ok, will you believe your dad and I were discussing friendship one day and he suggested that I get to know you? Next thing I knew, you dumped all your worldly possessions at my feet and invited me for supper."

She couldn't resist another objection. "People are never going to believe that we're just friends."

"Does it matter?" His eyes darkened again. "Leslie, I've spent enough time with your dad to understand that your family is struggling. Whether you want to admit it or not, the Leslie part of the family needs a friend to help her cope. I promise not to judge, advise, or blab."

She shook her head, lost in unbelief that he actually wanted to hang around. He started to pull away.

"No, I didn't mean no, I just mean—" She grabbed his arm. "I just can't believe you mean what you're saying."

"Kid, I've never meant anything more. I can't solve your problems, but if you'll let me, I'll try to make sure you don't have to figure them out solo." He hugged her again.

"Thanks," she whispered when he released her.

He looked at her intently for a moment, the mischief slowly lighting his eyes again. "I heard a rumor about oatmeal cake at my favorite professor's home. Shall we investigate?"

"Greedy." She tucked her hand back into the crook of his arm. "Dad will probably be home by the time we get there, so you'll have to share."

He smiled down at her and again covered her hand with his. They said little while they retraced their footprints, already half-obscured by new-fallen snow. How comforted Leslie felt by Dylan's presence, even when he didn't say anything. She glanced up at his profile. He caught her gaze, but only smiled.

six

From her place in the choir section Sunday morning, Leslie compared Mum's brown and cream sweater suit, French-braided hair, and pearl drop earrings with her own casual khaki wool dress and mousse-styled bangs. She couldn't remember Mum dressing up this much since Li'l Brad's dedication. Andrew slouched beside Mum, though some of his peers waved at him to join them. Brad and Karen sat on the other side of Mum with what appeared to be cheerful chatter.

Leslie couldn't believe her family's nonchalant, even cheerful, approach to this morning. Dad, wearing a cream V-necked sweater which matched Mum's outfit, greeted newcomers at the sanctuary door as though this day were nothing out of the ordinary. His lack of a suitcoat was as unusual as Mum's hairdo, though his dress shirt and tie preserved a Sunday-best image. He had repeatedly assured her that Mr. Smith's reading of his letter later this morning shouldn't be traumatic, but she didn't feel convinced. Maria or James undoubtedly would feel obligated to comment and offer pious reassurances of "prayer support". What a joke! They probably wouldn't be the only ones, either. How would Mum handle the inevitable gossip?

"Don't look so forlorn. You have at least one friend," a familiar voice whispered in her ear and a hand squeezed her shoulder.

She turned to Dylan, directly behind her. "Good morning to you, too." She smiled, noticing the sharp fit of his black two-piece suit accented with a green satin tie and pocket puff that matched his eyes. "How come I've never seen you in the choir before?"

"Maybe you're not observant. Everything all right?"

"I hope so." She noticed the choir director moving toward his music stand and turned herself around properly. Though she tried to concentrate on singing and the message, the dread in the pit of her stomach refused to disappear. What if someone tried to blame Andrew for Dad's decision? She forced her attention back to Pastor Quillan.

"I've cut my sermon short this morning because we have some family business to discuss. Those who do not wish to remain are free to leave. We're going to take a short break to allow choir members to find seats with their families. While we're moving around, I ask you to check your hearts carefully to ensure your motives for participating are to help and support members of our church family who are hurting."

Leslie picked up her Bible and purse. Would her suddenly trembly legs allow her to move? Dylan waited for her, calm encouragement in his expression. Andrew had moved over one seat so Dad could sit beside Mum. Leslie collapsed in the chair to Andrew's left. To her surprise, Dylan took the seat to her left. She felt too relieved by his support to care about what Karen would say if she noticed.

Pastor Quillan removed the microphone from its holder and walked down the platform steps. "Thank you to each one who has remained." His normally resonant voice had quieted to a gentle, conversational tone. "Before I ask Brother Smith to read you a letter that our deacons received this week, I want to give you an exhortation from the heart of your pastor and, I believe, from the heart of God. The letter which will be read to you in a few moments was prompted by circumstances of which only some of us may be aware. I'm sure none of us, save those involved, know the entirety of the situation. Along with our calling as brothers and sisters in Christ to bear one another's burdens comes temptation to use what little we know to gossip, often in the form of a prayer request or some religious cliche." He opened his Bible on the edge of the platform.

"It has been said that the Christian church is the only army which shoots its wounded. Experience shows me that gossip is the primary ammunition. Ephesians 4:29-32 explains how our Father feels about such unwholesome talk. I challenge you to say nothing to or about the family involved unless it is pure, unadulterated encouragement. They don't need our criticism and advice, only our love. Brother Smith?"

Leslie hadn't been aware her eyes overflowed until she felt something pressed into her hand. Where would she be without Dylan's handkerchiefs?

Ken Smith didn't take long to read Dad's simple letter. "God ordained the family thousands of years before He set up the church. From the beginning, He made it plain He holds the husband and father of each family responsible for that family's well-being. Our family has lately realized a need for us to intensify our commitment to one another. I am therefore asking to be released from the Heritage Christian Assembly Board of Deacons so I may invest my time more fully in my family." Mr. Smith paused to brush a hand across his eyes. He looked up from the letter.

"Anything I would try to add to what Brother Carlson has written here would be redundant. We as a board will miss his contribution, but I believe I speak for the entire board when I say we respect his commitment to his loved ones. The only way I can think of to communicate our love for this dear family is to have them all come forward so we can pray with them. You, too, Brad and Karen."

Leslie grasped Andrew's arm and followed her parents to the front, aware of many in the congregation wiping away tears. When Pastor Quillan asked for others to come forward in support, hardly anyone remained seated. Both the pastor and Mr. Smith prayed aloud. Then individuals made their way to speak to the Carlsons. Few said more than, "We love you" or "We're praying for you," accompanied by hugs or handshakes. By the time the crowd cleared, Leslie felt as limp as the soggy hanky she still clutched.

Dad, Mum, and Andrew stood off to one side, talking with Pastor Quillan. To Leslie's surprise, Brad and Karen had vanished. Dylan approached with her purse and Bible.

"Don't shoot—I'm not mugging you." From anyone else, the wacky humor would have been painfully inappropriate. But Dylan's eyes told her he wanted to ease her tension without disturbing her emotional fragility. "Your dad and I concocted a scheme before church. He and your Mum want to take Andrew out for lunch alone. It fits perfectly with my plan to take you out. Great minds, or what?"

Leslie couldn't help but grin. "What about Brad and

Karen?"

"Your dad just suggested that they might want to spend the afternoon as a family threesome."

"I'm surprised Karen went for it."

"Since your dad talked to Brad first, I don't think she had an option. I vote we not worry about them or anyone else. Let's just pretend to be a couple of selfish, irresponsible teenagers. Wait here and I'll bring the Princess around. There's a nasty wind out there." Dylan slung his grey wool coat on and pulled the collar up around his ears. Leslie watched him make his way to the car. A plume of exhaust confirmed he had again convinced the Princess to start. He hopped out quickly to brush new-fallen snow off the windows. When he finally pulled the car under the canopy in front of the doors, he opened the passenger door with a flourish.

"So, where are we going?" Leslie fastened her seat belt.

"Somewhere special." As usual, his teasing grin brought an answering smile to Leslie's face.

"I can handle being surprised." She wanted to chat charmingly with him, but felt too emotionally wrung out. He seemed to understand. He talked about inconsequential details, not saying anything demanding a reply, yet he paused often enough to give Leslie a chance to speak. She didn't say anything until they passed the last set of lights on the main highway out of town.

"I didn't know there were any restaurants out here."

"Drive long enough and you'll find one." He glanced at her with another easy smile.

"Right. Another ninety kilometers will have us in Riverview."

"You catch on quickly."

"You mean we're going to drive for an hour just to go out for lunch?"

"Unless it will mess up some heavy plans you have for the afternoon. Your dad said he didn't think you had anything going." He sounded worried.

"No, I'm just surprised."

He grinned like a little boy. "That's what I hoped for. Wait till you see where we're eating. I think they serve the best restaurant food in the North."

"This feels extravagant, driving so far just for a meal." Her delighted laugh showed she felt no offense.

"I want you to feel carefree, without a worry in the world."

His enthusiasm lifted Leslie's spirits. The church and her family receded like last month. Dylan told a funny story about one of his dorm buddies. It reminded Leslie of a prank one of the professors had pulled. Their laughter and stories lasted until Dylan stopped in front of a large brick building with a glassed-in sun porch beside a wide courtyard. An old-fashioned neon sign proclaimed "Papa Joe's."

"In the summer, they have umbrella tables scattered all over this area." Dylan gestured toward the courtyard with one hand and offered the other arm to Leslie. "The sun porch makes for better dining in winter."

She grasped his arm gratefully. She usually just wore her dress shoes outside on Sunday since Dad always let them out under the canopy at church. Though this parking lot had been well cleared, her brown alligator-skin high heeled pumps slipped on the snow. "You were right about the wind today. It seems worse here than at home."

"I don't think the wind ever stops blowing in Riverview.

That's one of several things I don't like about the town. Papa Joe's is one of the few things I do like."

Leslie gasped when they entered the restaurant. Mirrored tile on the ceiling made the wide open room seem even larger. Wooden and plush parrots of every size and color hung from the high ceiling over umbrella tables distributed thickly across a leaf-patterned carpet. Leslie couldn't see an unoccupied table.

"It's like a jungle." Her eyes widened delightedly. "Are you sure we can find a seat?"

"Absolutely." He smiled at an approaching waiter. "Reservation for two o'clock for Stoddard."

The waiter seated them in a corner of the sun porch, flourished menus in front of them, and chanted the specials. "I'll give you a moment to decide and be right back."

"These menus look like they were printed on paper bags." Leslie laughed.

"Papa Joe specializes in both good food and unusual effects. Pick anything you want. It's all delicious." Dylan seemed to be enjoying her delight.

"You've had it all?" She raised an eyebrow inquiringly.

"At one time or another. When we're on the rigs in this part of the world, no trip to town is complete without a meal at Papa Joe's."

"What's rig life like?"

"Rough, dirty, and hard work, but the pay is good. Though you do meet some real rough types." Dylan paused while the waiter took their order. The food arrived while he regaled her with anecdotes from his oil field experiences. Leslie ate between laughs, appreciating the exceptional flavor of her barbecued chicken. When she finished, Dylan insisted on dessert. They lingered over pie and several cups of tea.

A pause in the conversation gave Leslie the opening she had hoped for since their walk in the park. "Dylan, you mentioned something the other night about discovering your humanity need not disqualify you for the ministry. Would you mind explaining?"

He hesitated for several moments before he spoke. "I've never told anyone, other than my parents, but I'm glad you asked." He reached across the table to grasp her hand gently. To her surprise, she didn't want to pull away. "I've wanted to be a pastor ever since I can remember. As a small child, I was attracted to the idea of being able to yell in public without anyone telling me to be quiet. Typical kid, huh?"

Leslie responded with a smile. "So you've always been a nutcase?"

"Yep. Anyway, when I was around ten, a new pastor moved to our congregation. He and his wife were wonderful people, gentle, sympathetic, strong, wise—everything I thought a good pastor should be. They ran our youth group for awhile, giving me many opportunities to observe them informally and up close. Pastor Terry's encouragement reinforced my determination to be a pastor just like him.

"As it turned out, I had to work the year after high school in order to earn the money to pay for my dream. The month before I was due to start Bible School, our family faced a crisis that just about destroyed us all." His grip on her hand tightened and remembered pain glinted in his eyes.

"I, the aspiring pastor, left home without a forwarding address. I felt that if I could distance myself from my family's agony, my own pain might diminish. I'd been working for an oil company, so I simply asked to be sent out with a rig." He paused while the waiter re-filled their teapot.

"I spent the first six months in a state of exhaustion. I'd never done so much hard physical labor before and the effort of functioning kept my mind off my family. It turned out I had been assigned to Ken Smith's crew. Do you know he used to be a driller on the rigs?"

Leslie nodded. "He and Dad spent a lot of time together right after Ken hurt his back."

"Ken told me, and I knew who would be my favorite professor before I even met your dad." Dylan chuckled softly. "Anyway, Ken had been watching me from my first day on the job. Our first conversation consisted of him asking me why I wanted to work myself to death and my telling him to buzz off. Gradually, though, he got me to open up and before the year ended, I had restored contact with my family, though I had no intention of going home."

"Why not?" Leslie asked without thinking when he paused for a sip of tea. "I'm sorry. I don't mean to pry."

He smiled reassuringly and squeezed her hand. "You aren't. I'm glad you want to know. I didn't want to go home because I felt ashamed for running away. I kept thinking of Pastor Terry, how he was always there for hurting people in our congregation, and of the times he had been there for me. Since I was so obviously unfit for ministry, I decided that the rigs would be my career."

"What changed your mind?"

"Your dad."

"Dad? You didn't meet him until after you came to Bible School!" Leslie could tell by Dylan's grin he had anticipated her reaction.

"Actually I met him the year before in Ken's hospital room. Ken introduced me to your dad, then made the mistake of asking me how I was doing. I told him I was making good money, but I felt like I'd gotten lost. I was introducing my co-workers to the Lord, but I felt I was only doing half a job. I confided that for work that was supposed to be my career, the last eight years had been alarmingly long. Ken asked what I wanted to do. I told him of my dream. He asked why I hadn't pursued it. I blurted out my feelings of inferiority and failure. At that point, your dad asked me if I'd ever heard of David."

Leslie smiled. "I should have known. Sometimes I wonder if Dad knows about anyone else in Scripture." She stifled a yawn. Though she wanted the conversation to continue indefinitely, she could feel her lack of sleep from the last several nights.

"He took me out for lunch and showed me in Scripture every guy who failed and what God did with them afterward. He didn't preach, he just answered my questions with biblical illustrations. I wasn't so much impressed with his knowledge of Scripture as with his ability to apply it practically. Listening to him even now makes me see people in the Bible as real people, rather than superheroes."

"He taught us kids the same way, and I've always felt privileged." This time the yawn escaped. "Sorry. It's really not the company. I just haven't slept well lately, and it's catching up with me."

"Not to worry." Dylan squeezed her hand again. "You're relaxing and that's my objective. How about if we head for home, and I'll shut up so you can sleep." He helped her into her coat, squeezing her shoulders gently before reaching for his wallet.

"Maybe the fresh air will wake me up," she suggested hopefully. Yet, despite her best intentions, the gentle motion of the car made Leslie's eyes heavy even before they reached the highway back to Nipson.

Dylan stretched his arm across the back of the seat. "There's a blanket in the back you can wad up for a pillow, if you like, or you can use my shoulder."

Just the thought of reaching for the blanket required more energy than Leslie felt ready to expend. "I don't mean to be rude," she mumbled, and let her head rest against his arm.

"Go ahead and sleep, Les. I'll keep track of the world for you." He grinned and gently pulled her over to lean on his shoulder.

She probably shouldn't get so close to him. She'd think about that later when she didn't feel so sleepy. For now, she felt safe and comforted.

seven

Leslie wearily stacked dishes. She had at least four hours of studying to do this weekend, but she didn't feel energetic enough to finish cleaning the kitchen. The week had been exhausting. Though Andrew's general attitude had improved, he remained remote. Mum's health had continued to decline to the point that she spent most of every day in bed. Gossip had yet to surface according to Leslie's expectations, but she still felt she moved through each day in the cocoon of her family's problems, not really participating in what others considered normal daily life.

Now it appeared the cocoon would swallow her usually excellent grades. Leslie tried to remember the last time she had felt prepared for a class. Lately her evenings had filled up with some family discussion or Dylan. He always managed to be on hand when needed. His perception of her moods had gradually become comforting, rather than threatening.

Dad's call from his study interrupted Leslie's daze. She hurried to him, and he looked up with a smile. "Have a sit. What do you think of Andrew's behavior lately?"

"He seems to have calmed down, though I haven't studied him closely. I've been so relieved he hasn't been avoiding us or creating confrontations I've tried to leave well enough alone."

"Leslie?"

She forced herself to look him in the eyes, and hated

herself for the emotions he probably saw in hers. He held out his arms, inviting her to sit on his lap. "You sure you want to do this?" she tried to joke. "It would be embarrassing to have to explain to the doctor how you broke your leg."

"I'm not as delicate as all that, Daughter." He hugged her tightly. "I think we need to talk about you. I appreciate your efforts to keep our family running as smoothly as possible and to keep your feelings from burdening us. But, Leslie, you're part of the family, too. I'd like to talk with Joanne and Andrew about helping you around the house."

Leslie opened her mouth to argue, but Dad kept talking. "I'd also like you take the rest of the day off. I know you have a list as long as your arm of things you think you need to do, but the world won't come to an end if you don't do it. If you feel you must do something, you may study. But try to relax, nap if you can. You're a wonderful daughter, but you're not Superwoman." He pushed her gently off his lap and steered her toward the door. "For starters, promise me you'll spend an hour lying down. Please?"

Leslie nodded and stumbled up the stairs, too discouraged even for tears. A nap? Hah! She knew her mind would simply race with innumerable details. In addition to the usual round of cooking, cleaning, laundry, and studying, a surprise party had to be planned for Andrew after his last game of the season next weekend, and Vince's room cleaned for his visit at the same time.

Leslie pulled the blind over her window and snuggled under her favorite blanket. Hmmm. Just lying here did feel good. Funny how people kept sending her to bed. Leslie grinned wryly, recalling Granny's visit a couple of evenings ago. The dear lady had arrived unannounced with Mr. Smith and declared her intention to "make myself useful while Ken visits with your dad." She had then recommended Leslie treat herself to a long bubble bath and an early bedtime. Remembering, Leslie felt tension drain out of her muscles. Granny had also suggested she recruit family assistance with some of the chores consuming her study time. Maybe Dad's idea would work.

Her mind drifted to Dylan. Hopefully he'd call later. Leslie slept, dreaming of smiling green eyes.

A soft tap on her door woke her. "Leslie?" Andrew's voice called softly. "It's supper time."

Supper? She sat up groggily, trying to orient herself. Slowly she recalled her chat with Dad. Right, he had sent her to take a nap. Her bedside clock showed 5:06 p.m. She quickly brushed her hair into a ponytail and almost tripped over a pile of clean, folded clothes in the hallway. What on earth! Maybe she hadn't come out of her dream yet.

Dad and Andrew stood at attention in the kitchen, swathed in huge white aprons and wearing goofy paper hats. "Escort her to the table, Boss," Andrew ordered grandly. With a flourish, Dad extended his elbow and guided Leslie into the dining room. Tablecloth, candles, china, cloth napkins.

"You guys sure went all out." She felt awkward as the focus of attention. "Mum! I'm glad you're up. Feeling better?"

Mum smiled like a small child trying to keep a secret. "Much better, dear. And you? Dad said you were feeling a little ragged."

"He sent me upstairs for a nap four hours ago. I can't believe I slept that long!"

"Not to worry." Dad placed a dish of scalloped potatoes

and ham on a hot pad. "You must have needed the rest. As you can see, we have things well under control. You will be a lady of leisure for the rest of the evening."

Leslie watched while Dad and Andrew loaded the table with dishes of steamed broccoli, garlic bread, fruit salad, tossed salad and pitchers containing juice and ice water. "I never would have guessed you guys had it in you," she said with amazement.

"Hey, our talents are nothing short of incredible." Andrew poured tea into the cup near her plate. "Just wait until you see dessert."

"So which Good Fairy finished the laundry?" Leslie inquired when Dad finished the blessing.

"The same lady who also changed the sheets and dusted Vince's room," Dad informed her.

"You didn't have to do that, Mum," Leslie felt overwhelmed. "You haven't been feeling so hot yourself."

Mum smiled self-consciously. "It wasn't a big deal. I came out around 3:00 to find these two in the kitchen whispering and stirring around, and I wanted to get in on the action."

Leslie tasted her food. "These scalloped potatoes are terrific! Where did you guys find the ham?"

"We'll never tell." Andrew winked at her.

The food disappeared in record time. Dad and Andrew cleared the table amid laughter and jokes. Suddenly the kitchen fell quiet. Leslie looked at Mum, who just smiled. Dad and Andrew appeared in the doorway, each carrying an end of a cake plate which held an angel food cake topped with whipped cream.

"This is your favorite, isn't it, Les?" Andrew inquired with a worried frown.

"Yes, but if it weren't, I'd still be thrilled at all the effort you guys have gone to." Leslie didn't know whether to laugh or cry.

"Compared with what you do for us all the time, it's not much," Dad said, looking at her meaningfully. "Hopefully this will even things out a bit." He placed a piece of white cardboard beside her plate.

"What's this?" She studied it, noting its list of housekeeping jobs accompanied by initials.

"It's our attempt to put our family back in balance." Dad resumed his seat at the head of the table. "In a nutshell, I'm in charge of dishes every night, including breakfast dishes if I can convince you to leave them for me. Andrew's offered to make his own lunches and help keep the upstairs bathroom tidy. Mum and I will take care of our own suite and the downstairs bathroom, and she's offered to take the laundry off your hands permanently. Everyone's responsible for scrounging lunch on Saturdays so you don't have to cook. Since our efforts were so successful tonight, Andrew and I will handle Thursday and Saturday suppers every week. Any comments?"

"Looks like a good plan." Leslie didn't feel sure it would work.

"Hey, don't look so worried, Les." Andrew's eyes appeared amazingly clear and cheerful. "Bathroom cleanup sounds gross, but I can handle it. And I won't just put Snickers bars and coke in my lunches. I know the formula—sandwich, raw veggy, a piece of fruit and a dessert." He grinned smugly.

She met his smile with an affectionate shake of her head. He always met every new project with enthusiasm that often dwindled to disinterest in a few days.

"Thanks, Son." Dad looked from Leslie to Andrew. "I trust you realize you've committed to a five-days-a-week job. In other words, I'd better not catch Leslie making lunches again this year. Understood by you both?" The affection in his eyes kept his words from sounding like an elementary school lecture. "Now, who wants dessert?"

Dad and Andrew shooed Leslie out of the kitchen while they did dishes. She wandered to Dad's study, feeling disoriented. Though her family's help would be welcome, she felt guilty relinquishing so much responsibility. She studied the books lining one wall, absently wondering if any of them would provide help.

"Les?"

She turned to face Dad, who positioned himself in the easy chair near his desk. "Sit here, hon." He patted the arm. "You're still not comfortable with our schedule."

Leslie shook her head.

"I know we've discussed this before, but let me try again. Responsibility is a good thing. But you're allowing it to become a compulsion. Mum and Andrew will let you take over as much as you want to. You're not doing them any favors. This is a time of adjustment and growth for all of us. You need to let them grow, too. Besides, you need to make time for yourself."

"It sounds good," Leslie agreed. "But it doesn't feel right."

Dad seemed to think about her comment for a few moments. "Try this analogy. When you've been sitting on the floor for awhile, your legs go numb, right? When you get up, it hurts. Does that mean you shouldn't walk?"

Leslie shook her head again.

"The reason your legs hurt is that you were using them

improperly before you tried to walk. It's not the walking but the previous use that created the problem. In the same way, your caring instincts have been abused. Now that we've decided to redirect them, you may feel unbalanced for awhile. Remember, it's not your feelings or your current activities that are creating the problem. It's the bad habits we've helped you develop."

Leslie mentally viewed a tiny light in the cloud of guilt enveloping her. She wandered back to the bookshelf.

"How are your studies?"

"All right, I guess."

"According to a professor who thinks you're his prize student, that's not quite accurate." Dad's eyes revealed no reproach. "Arthur Jonas told me Friday he's worried about you. Something about not passing a quiz?"

Leslie had to think for a moment before she realized who Dad was talking about. Professor seemed a much more appropriate first name for her geography teacher than Arthur. "I know he makes his quizzes difficult, but I just had no time to study. I squeaked through a couple of weeks ago and thought I could do it again."

"Are you sleeping okay?"

"Not really," Leslie admitted.

"Let me guess. Your mind's going like a whirlwind trying to balance everything you have to do against your academic needs, not to mention your concern for Andrew."

"And Mum."

Dad's eyebrows lifted ominously. "Apparently this conversation is long overdue." The love in his voice belied his thunderous expression. "Leslie Joanne! I appreciate your loyalty to Mum and your desire to protect her. But taking care of Mum is *my* job."

Tears flooded Leslie's eyes too fast for her to blink them away. Dad walked to her and wrapped his arms around her. "Honey, I'm worried about Andrew, too. I also understand your concern for your mum. But if you don't put down some of your burdens, you'll wear out and won't be any good for anything. If you can't do it for yourself, will you do it for me?"

"How?"

"For starters, take care of *yourself.* Make adequate rest your first priority, your studies second, and your family fourth." A smile warmed his voice.

Leslie pondered his suggestions. Something didn't sound right. First, second— An answering smile tugged at her lips when she looked at him. "And what's third?"

"I'll let you figure that out on your own."

eight

"Sounds like a great idea, Dylan. Let me check with Dad." Leslie braced her knee against the wall, balanced the laundry basket on her leg, cupped her hand over the mouthpiece of the phone and directed her voice toward the open door of the study. "Dad? Dylan would like to take me skating around 8:00 tonight. Will that interfere with any of your plans?"

Dad poked his head around the corner of the doorway. "Sounds great to me. Tell him it's worth more points on the next exam if he takes me to A&W instead."

Leslie made a face at him and addressed the phone again. "Dylan? Dad's all in favor, though he says treating him to A&W will earn you more points." She could hear Dylan's delighted laugh.

"You can tell Professor Carlson mere points won't compensate for leaving his daughter behind. I'll see ya' later tonight, kid. Don't forget to dress warmly."

Leslie hung up the phone and folded herself into a sitting position on the floor. She leaned her chin on her arms folded across the laundry basket in her lap. Something extra had been in Dylan's voice tonight, something that made her feel warm all over, even a little lightheaded.

"Watch it, Carlson," she warned herself. "You've found a great friend. Don't go mucking it up with a bunch of romantic imaginations." She studied the rumpled towels sternly as though they were to blame for her unsteady emotions. Mum had managed to do a bit of laundry this week, but she'd requested help today. *At least you don't have to iron Dad's shirts or fuss with Andrew's gym socks,* Leslie reminded herself. What should she wear this evening?

Four hours later, the question remained unanswered, though she only had thirty minutes until Dylan's arrival. Time for action. She pulled on sweat pants, which she topped with a pair of thick tan corduroy pants. A brown turtleneck and a green, gold, and brown sweater topped the outfit. Her ears would stay warmer if she left her hair loose, so she brushed it well and pulled it away from her face with a green terry headband. She fluffed and curled her bangs then selected dangly gold earrings. Her make-up presented a challenge. Should she bother with eye shadow? A light dusting of green would darken her hazel eyes to almost brown, but would it be too dressy for skating? Who cares, she decided. She felt like wearing the shadow, so she would. A quick squirt of perfume and she felt ready.

Anticipation sent her dancing down the stairs. Somehow just being around Dylan made her feel like a different person. Not exactly different, perhaps, but definitely special. She pulled out the miscellaneous winter wear box from its place in the entry. There should be a green hat here just the color of her sweater. Her brown mittens would match the brown scarf she pulled from the box as the doorbell rang.

Dylan's mischievous grin greeted her when she opened the door. "Fancy meeting you here," he quipped and gave her a quick hug. "You look fashionable. Sure you want to go skating with a rag bag like me?"

Leslie glanced over his apparel, forcing her most thoughtful expression. Dylan had also selected corduroy pants, but his were brown. A green polo shirt emphasized the green flecks in his tan sweater, which in turn emphasized his green eyes. "Guess you'll do," she responded, reminding herself not to be so aware of his eyes. Green eyes were green eyes, right? *Wrong*, she acknowledged.

"You look like you're thinking something I'd like to know about," Dylan observed. "A penny for your thoughts, or are they worth more these days?"

Leslie's face felt baptized in heat and Dylan laughed. "I take it by your vibrant blush, we should change the subject."

Leslie didn't want to mess up her hair, so she stuffed her hat into the pocket of her coat. She slung the scarf around her neck, pulled on her boots, and grabbed her skates. The process gave her face time to return to normal.

"Ready when you are." She turned to face Dylan.

"Then let's split. Should you have some extra support on this slippery snow?" He extended his hand. His twinkling eyes told her he knew the snow wouldn't be that treacherous, but he wanted contact.

Leslie returned his smile and accepted his offer. His affectionate smile warmed her all over, but also left a trembly feeling in her stomach. "And how was your day?" she asked to get the mood on to safer ground.

He helped her into the car, which he had left running, before answering. "After I finished my Pastoral Counselling assignment, rather boring. I've discovered that unless I take corrective measures, Saturdays can be a real drag."

"Why?" Leslie wondered if he had been assigned particularly miserable dorm chores.

"There's a certain redheaded friend I get to spend time with every other day of the week except Saturdays—unless, of course, I can concoct an excuse to change things."

Leslie didn't know how to respond. So the extra something in his voice earlier today hadn't been her imagination. Excitement and apprehension chased each other along her spine.

Dylan didn't try to resurrect conversation until they reached the skating rink behind the high school. He paused before turning off the ignition. "You're awfully quiet all of a sudden." He again reached for her hand. "Did I say something I shouldn't have?"

"No." Leslie tried to figure out which of her feelings to put into words. She settled for, "I've just never had a friend like you."

Dylan removed his hand, but continued looking at her. "It's all right to feel uncertain, provided you don't let fright send you into hiding. I told you I want to be your friend. I've developed an affection for you that could easily become more than friendship. When the time is right for that, we'll both know, and the questions will answer themselves. For now, our focus is getting you through your current challenges. Friends?" He extended a gloved hand for a handshake.

Both Dylan's gesture and his explanation reminded her how safe he had proven to be. She shook his hand solemnly. "Thanks."

He turned off the car and hurried to her side to help her out. "With that settled, milady, let's find out what these skates can do."

Stars twinkled overhead and several street lights lit the

skating area. Leslie and Dylan seated themselves on a rough wooden bench. From her first skating experience at six years old, Leslie had loved gliding over the ice. The controlled slide gave her a feeling of grace.

"Catch me if you can," she called over her shoulder. Dylan remained on the bench, struggling with his laces.

"Enjoy your head start," he shouted back. "I'll be right behind you in a moment."

Leslie propelled herself with short, firm strokes. She rounded the fourth curve of the oval with enough speed to coast past the bench where Dylan still sat. She stared into the sky, relishing its infinity.

A commotion to her right grabbed her attention. Dylan had lost his balance as his skate blades contacted ice rather than packed snow. Leslie tried not to laugh as his arms gyrated wildly while his feet seemed to have a mind of their own. To his credit, he didn't fall down. He scowled at Leslie. "Your papa never taught you not to laugh at people in trouble?" He twitched his shoulders indignantly and went down in a heap.

With a chuckle, Leslie rushed to help him. "You didn't tell me you don't know how to skate!"

"I still haven't." He panted from exertion and clutched Leslie's arm with both hands. "My skates just haven't learned who's boss. Hey! Where are you going?"

Leslie continued moving slowly, dragging Dylan with her. "You won't learn by standing there. Relax and get used to balancing yourself. I'll provide the momentum."

"Relax the woman says. I'm used to having size twelves planted firmly on the ground and she wants me to relax while balanced on a quarter inch of steel without a tread in sight."

Though he grumbled, Leslie could feel his grip on her arm easing. "Try grabbing my hands instead," she suggested. "I'll skate backwards."

"Showoff," he muttered, then grinned. "I really did know how to do this. It's just been awhile."

"Like how long?"

"Grade three."

She bit back a grin. His efforts to stay standing resembled Li'l Brad pulling himself up on furniture. "Why did you quit?"

"It had nothing to do with coordination," he blustered. The words were barely out of his mouth when his feet slid out from under him.

"I wouldn't think such a thing!" Leslie laughed. His spread-eagle posture on the ice contrasted sharply with his usual confident demeanor. She pulled him upright again. "Tell me why this area of your education got neglected."

"It's this way," he began as his skates wobbled again. This time he controlled the slide and stayed standing. "Until I was ten, we lived in a house that bordered the playground of an elementary school. They flooded part of it in the winter to make a skating rink. But then we moved to a subdivision and I found other things to amuse myself."

"I find this quite amusing." Leslie couldn't help herself.

"I'm sure you do," he responded, though his grin told her he took no offense.

They took another circuit around the rink before Leslie tried disengaging her hands. "Ok, now stand on your own."

Panic flitted across Dylan's face. He braced his feet before letting go with one hand.

Leslie smiled reassuringly. "Don't lock your knees or

you'll go down again. Just stand with your weight on the balls of your feet. Now transfer your weight to your left foot and use the edge of your right skate blade to push gently."

He still clutched her hand, but followed her instructions. He slid forward a fraction of an inch before locking his knees. Leslie grabbed his arm before he lost his balance. "Don't fight the motion. Lean into it. Try again."

Gradually Dylan's shaky movements developed rhythm. He skated all the way around the rink without Leslie's support, though she hovered close by. "Now that I've proven I can do it, will you let me hold on?"

She grinned and offered an arm. Though assisting Dylan meant she didn't experience the free grace of movement she usually associated with skating, she still enjoyed herself.

"Miss Carlson. Fancy meeting you here. I would have thought you would be studying for your repeat exam." James Trindle's unmistakable tones intruded on her thoughts.

Leslie had been so absorbed in Dylan's skating she hadn't noticed new arrivals. Maria stood near her brother, and other acquaintances from the Bible School zipped around the rink laughing and shouting. She tried to formulate a neutral reply.

But James lectured on with his usual disregard for her input. "I do hope Mr. Stoddard is not the cause for your delinquency."

Leslie supposed his smirk was supposed to pass for a friendly smile. Instead, it fueled her indignation. "I believe I told you at our last encounter, James, that when I want your opinion I will ask for it. Excuse us, please."

She propelled herself quickly past them, dragging Dylan along. "One of these days that jerk is going to realize I don't care what he thinks!"

Dylan let go of her arm. "Time out."

Leslie suddenly realized she had been skating much faster than his skill allowed. "Sorry. I'm not paying attention."

"That's okay. How about taking a couple of turns around the rink as fast as you want, and we can talk about things when you get back. I'll practice standing while you're gone."

Leslie smiled gratefully and skated off quickly. Her usual frustration with James had been exacerbated tonight by his public announcement of her academic problems. She wished she were strong enough to blacken his eye, choke him—anything to obliterate his smug expression.

She waved to Dylan as she passed. He seemed to be adjusting to his skates, and had even managed to skate around to the far side of the rink. The next time she approached, he seemed to be talking with James, who skated backward easily while conversing—or rather, taunting, Leslie realized when she got close enough to eavesdrop.

". . . haven't skated before, Mr. Stoddard. It's an important part of our recreational life in this part of the world."

Dylan inclined his head in silent acknowledgment. Leslie wished she could see his face. She slowed down so as not to interrupt.

"Of course there's a lot a city fellow wouldn't know about life in humble little Nipson. Slick city manners can't replace hard work and the committed friendships that are forged here in the North."

Leslie wanted to laugh at an aspiring egghead telling a roughneck about hard work. She moved a little closer to hear Dylan's reply. "You have a point, I assume?" Though his voice sounded friendly, Leslie had never before heard the chill underlying his tone.

"Since you've asked for my advice, I'll keep it short and simple."

"Which would be a first," Leslie muttered under her breath.

"Those of us in the Heritage church family are quite concerned for the Carlson family, which has been deeply shamed by young Andrew's recent behavior. I, for one, will not take kindly to anyone complicating Miss Carlson's life. She has some difficult decisions to make and will be best helped by —"

Leslie started moving as soon as she heard Andrew's name. Two quick strides brought her close enough to slap James' face as hard as she could. With the slap came deadly calm. "I'll be best helped by you shutting your mouth."

James' eyes widened in shock. He stared at Leslie for a moment, his hand slowly rising to his reddened cheek. "Miss Carlson, I was only trying to —"

"To meddle and force your bigoted opinions where they aren't welcome. When it comes to being a friend, Dylan knows more than you're capable of understanding. How about if you shut up for a change? You might learn something." Her voice quavered and her legs trembled. "Dylan, I'm ready to go home."

She focused on the ground as they moved to the bench. "I shouldn't have done that," she mumbled. "But his insinuations made me boil." She unlaced her skates with sharp jerks.

When Dylan replied, his voice still held that unfamiliar chill. "Leslie, you're not the one who —"

"Mr. Stoddard, I want you to know that I hold you completely responsible for Miss Carlson's totally unchristian behavior." James strutted off the ice to plant himself directly in front of Dylan. "I have never known her to be anything other than the gracious, gentle woman Scripture directs her to be. Her vulgar display —"

For the second time that evening, action interrupted James. Dylan erupted from the bench. Heedless of the skates he still wore, he took a step toward James, who instinctively backed up. Dylan reached for James' lapels. James extended both hands to stop him. Dylan shoved the arms aside, unbalancing the shorter man. James flailed his arms to regain his footing, backing toward the skating rink. When Dylan continued to approach, James turned to flee. He tripped over his own feet and crashed face-first onto the skating area. Leslie heard the unmistakable crunch of breaking glass.

Dylan's face remained frozen in a grim mask. He strode back to the bench and changed his footwear. Wordlessly, he guided Leslie to the car.

"Dylan?" Leslie touched his arm uncertainly.

His face softened as he looked at her, placing one of his hands over hers. "I guess it's my turn to apologize."

"For what? I thought you exercised remarkable restraint. Better than I did."

"Thanks for your confidence. Thanks, too, for the compliment earlier. I hope my temper didn't change your opinion."

"Compliment?" The evening's details had already grown fuzzy in Leslie's memory.

"You told our friend that he could take lessons from me in friendship."

"He could learn from you in many ways, Dylan. A lot of guys could." Leslie couldn't interpret Dylan's expression in the dim light. He seemed to be analyzing something while he looked at her. Without a word, he started the car.

He didn't speak until they reached her home and he walked her to the door. Then he only said, "Thanks, Leslie."

nine

The Nipson Bearcats won the championship. After the game, the Carlson family gathered to celebrate. Leslie found a cheerful smile before she faced the group in the living room. Seeing Karen and Brad snuggle on the love seat reminded her of the last family gathering—except Dylan had been on the piano bench, not Vince. Andrew had missed that one, too.

"Mmm. Cracker things!" Brad grabbed a handful off the tray. "Did you make these just for me?"

"They're called cream cheese hors d'oeuvres, and I did make them with you in mind. Just share, okay?"

"That spoils his fun." Karen laughed. "He's not used to having competition at the table."

"Wait till Li'l Brad turns twelve," Dad predicted.

"Where's your boyfriend, Les? He gave me a run for my money last time."

Leslie tried to keep her tone light. "If you're referring to Dylan, he had to study."

"Boyfriend?" Vince's eyebrows lifted mischievously. "Have I heard about this?"

"I told you about Dylan in the letter which you never answered. He's just a friend."

"That's probably a good way to keep it," Karen offered. "He's quite a bit older than you, isn't he?"

"A bit," Leslie replied, hoping desperately someone would change the subject. For some reason she couldn't fathom, Karen's comment had pushed her alarmingly close to tears.

Vince seemed to perceive her wish, but his efforts didn't improve the situation. "Speaking of the men in your life, what do you hear from James Trindle?"

Karen didn't give her a chance to reply. "He kept a pretty low profile last week at church. I heard a rumor that Leslie had something to do with it." Her eyes sparkled with interest.

Vince grinned. "Did you actually puncture his delusions of grandeur?"

"We just had a discussion and he embarrassed himself."

Brad whistled. "Mr. Perfection embarrassed himself? Let me guess, that's when he threw his glasses to the ground in disgust."

Dad stepped into the conversation. "As long as we're discussing love interests, how are you faring in that department, Vince? Have you found yourself a gorgeous redhead yet?" He put his arm around Mum.

A light blush crept up Vince's neck and ears. "Not particularly," he hedged.

Brad's face lit with glee. He wrapped his hand around Karen's. "I'll bet she's a petite blonde. So tell us all about her."

Leslie admired Vince's composure. Other than the telltale red around his ears, he remained unreadable. "There are plenty of options—stunning brunettes, gorgeous redheads, beautiful blondes. Variety, you know."

"I also know what Proverbs says about rejoicing with the wife of your youth. Won't be long before you're too late for that." Dad's grin matched Brad's for mischief.

"Speaking of youth, where's the infant?" Vince looked

around with mock concern, appearing unaware he'd changed the subject.

As if on cue, a wail sounded from Dad and Mum's bedroom. Karen's eyes sparkled. "Would the fond uncle like to bring his nephew out here?"

"Don't fall for it, Vince," Brad warned. "After the nap is major soggy diaper time. You haven't seen wrath until you hand Karen a wet baby."

"Thanks for the warning, pal. I'm practically a stranger to him, anyway. He'd probably appreciate it if someone familiar got him up." Vince's face provided a study in innocence.

"Men!" Karen spluttered.

"Let me do it," Mum offered, rising. "I've changed enough diapers in my time. It's actually simpler than these big, brave men think it is."

Leslie looked at Dad in surprise. This was the first time in months Mum had participated in family teasing. Dad watched Mum leave, a pleased smile lighting his eyes.

By 8:00 Leslie's disappointment at Andrew's absence had turned to alarm. When Brad and Karen left an hour later due to Li'l Brad's fussiness, Leslie breathed easier. Karen's presence could have made whatever lay ahead much worse.

Mum went to bed right after hugging Li'l Brad goodbye. Vince disappeared, probably to his room. Dad joined Leslie in the kitchen to help with clean-up.

"Glad to have your big brother home?" His eyes twinkled, though Leslie saw a mist of worry there, too.

"I'd be gladder if my little brother were also home."

"It doesn't feel good to me, either. But what can we do except wait?"

Leslie smiled wryly and kept stacking dishes. It wouldn't help to verbalize what they both were thinking.

Dad also did his part in silence, washing plates, glasses, cups and cutlery. Eventually, he let the water out of the sink, carefully hanging the wash cloth over the oven door handle.

"Dylan does that, too," Leslie commented before she could stop herself.

"Does what?"

"Hangs the dish cloth where it can dry. I noticed it the first time he visited."

"That was Li'l Brad's birthday party, wasn't it?" Dad seemed to be watching her reaction.

She nodded, not attempting to conceal her feelings. Dad knew her too well for it to work.

"Is it my imagination or has the phone been conspicuous by its silence this week?"

His gentle inquiry made her eyes sting with tears she didn't want to release. "He's been avoiding me at school, too. I have a hunch it has something to do with what happened with James, but I can't figure out what."

"I could tell you haven't been comfortable discussing that scene, but would you mind telling me about it?" Dad leaned against the cupboard with his hands in his jeans pockets.

She recounted the events for him, including her reactions. "I've never seen James so antagonistic," she finished. "I've also never seen myself react to him that way. I can usually consider the source and let it pass."

"Did you and Dylan discuss what had happened?"

"No. We each apologized for messing up the evening and drove home in silence. I had no idea the silence would last this long."

"Do you want my interpretation?"

She faced him with a smile of relief. "Please. You know him a lot better than I do."

Dad didn't say anything until Leslie finished putting the dishes away. He looked her straight in the eyes. "I think James sparked some unfamiliar reactions in both of you. Perhaps Dylan is trying to sort out his feelings while you're alternately trying to understand and ignore yours. Both acknowledging what you feel and letting him analyze himself requires trust on your part. That trust makes the difference between mere acquaintanceship and a meaningful friendship."

Leslie's first coherent thought turned audible before she could stop it. "That sounds heavier than I want to think about."

Dad opened his arms for a hug. "That's why you're as strong as you are, Les. You aren't afraid to tackle what you don't want to face. You're like Mum in many ways. But as long as you maintain this approach, you'll never find life to be more than you can handle."

His praise momentarily overwhelmed Leslie. She knew his comparison of her with Mum represented one of the highest compliments he could give.

Dad smiled encouragingly. "How about a game with Vince while we wait for Andrew?"

They decided on something similar to dominoes played with triangular tiles. Vince had just won his sixth round when the door banged open. Leslie felt a chill that had nothing to do with the sub-zero air rushing in. She almost ran to the entry.

"Hiyah, Les. Anybody show you my trophy?" Andrew

held a large object aloft. His eyes looked overbright and he lurched slightly in the doorway. The door remained wide open behind him.

Leslie tried to focus on the trophy. "What's it say?"

"Dunno. Something about playin' good. I hope Vinsh tripsh over it." Andrew's words started to slur. He appeared to try to steady himself by talking slowly. "Now . . . maybe he won't . . .think he'sh . . ." Andrew paused and tried again. ". . . think he's . . . the only shmart . . . smart one." He almost spat his s sounds, trying to make them clear. The extra air behind his words increased the odor of beer.

Leslie looked behind her at Vince coming out of the den. His eyes burned with anger. Dad put a restraining hand on Vince's shoulder. "Don't say anything, please," he whispered. He motioned Leslie aside so he and Andrew faced each other directly.

"Have you been drinking, son?"

"Yep. And this time Coach can't do nuthin' cuz the sheason'sh over. It wush a good party." Andrew tried to swagger and almost fell.

Dad reached out quickly to steady him. "How did you get home?"

"Tom let me drive. Pretty neat car."

Dad's voice sounded ominous. "How much did Tom drink?"

"Dunno. 'Sh none of my bushnish."

"Well, son, it is my business how much you drink. Coming home this late in this condition tells me something about your sense of responsibility. I told you your sister wanted to have a family dinner tonight."

"Sorry, Leelee." Andrew leaned against the wall as if

bored.

"Hand me your driver's license, please." Dad held out his hand. A mulish expression settled over Andrew's features. Dad spoke again firmly, but quietly. "Right now."

Not moving his gaze from Dad's face, Andrew fumbled around his pockets until he retrieved his wallet. He opened it, then seemed to lose track of what he was doing. He started to put it on the hallway table by the phone.

"Your driver's license, son." Dad didn't move.

Andrew withdrew the small plastic card and tried to slap it into Dad's hand but missed. Dad quietly took it from his fingers.

"Take yourself up to bed and we'll talk about this in more detail tomorrow." Andrew started unsteadily up the stairs, but halted when Dad spoke again. "You will get up in time to join us for church."

Leslie wanted to follow him, but Dad stopped her. "He drew a battle line tonight. I'm going to ensure he experiences the consequences of that decision. If you really love him, Les, you won't try to shield him."

The pain in his eyes stopped her from protesting. She looked over his shoulder to Vince whose face showed shock.

"Vinny?" She used her childhood name for him, hoping to steady him.

"I'm okay. I think I'll go to bed now." He stoically walked to his room next to the den. His door shut with a slow click.

Leslie found herself in Dad's arms again. The feel of moisture on her neck caused her to look up into his face, where tears streamed.

"Oh, Les." He let his head fall forward onto her shoulder and she barely heard his muffled words. "I'd prayed this wouldn't have to happen."

ten

Leslie remembered little of Sunday's events. Instead, the day blanketed her memory with a crazy quilt of emotions. Apprehension when Dad called the family to breakfast. Empathy for Andrew's misery, reflected in his grey-green pallor and frequent wincing at the normal sounds of family life. Frustration with Vince's sullen silence. Disappointment at Dylan's absence from church. Leslie knew he had probably left for home right after classes on Friday, but she'd hoped to see him anyway.

She allowed herself to sleep in Monday morning. Though she had much she wanted to accomplish during spring break, she'd determined to take time for extra rest. The house seemed oddly silent when she awoke. She hurried downstairs in her bathrobe to investigate. Wandering down the hallway, she peered into Vince's empty room. She moved to the kitchen window. Vince had evidently decided to shovel the snow off the back deck. He tossed a big scoop onto the rapidly growing pile with almost-frantic energy.

Leslie's unease intensified. She'd been looking forward to Vince's return, counting on his psychology studies to give her some insight into Andrew's behavior. Instead Vince's behavior had become a mystery of its own. She stumbled back upstairs to shower and dress. A glance at Andrew's room revealed nothing but the familiar closed door. About 10:30, Dad spoke softly from her doorway.

"May I come in?"

She looked up and beckoned. He pulled the chair away from her desk and settled into it like a weary laborer at the end of a 14-hour shift. "I've been talking to our Father since Saturday evening and I think He's given me direction. I'd like your input." His face still looked drawn, though his eyes had regained life. They weren't twinkling as usual, but at least they no longer looked dull and pain-filled. He paused for her reaction.

"Okay." She pulled a nearby pillow into her lap to hide the trembling in her hands.

"I think the end of basketball season also signals the end of whatever control Andrew kept over himself after his suspension. I don't know yet what's motivating him toward alcohol. I don't even know how strong an attraction it holds for him. I do know only he can make the choice to refuse to drink. About the best we can do is back off and let him experience the consequences of his choice." Dad paused and looked at her intently.

"You're saying he'll get worse?" Leslie wrapped her arms around the pillow and hugged it tightly against the pain that grabbed her middle.

"I wouldn't be surprised. That's why I wanted to talk to you." His brown eyes conveyed tenderness. "His behavior the other night shocked us, and we're all still reeling. What came to me yesterday, though, is that we'd better prepare ourselves for worse and determine that we won't be lured into his emotional responses. If we're not careful, he'll soon control the entire family with his behavior."

Leslie protested, hardly aware she'd spoken her thoughts. "But Andrew's not like that." She visualized his lopsided grin and awkward hugs.

Dad said nothing for several moments, just stared through the window behind Leslie. Slowly he pulled his gaze back to her face. "Leslie, have you let yourself realize Andrew may be addicted to alcohol?"

She stared, horrified Dad had actually said it. "We don't know that for sure!"

"Maybe it's time we read the signals. I've been doing a bit of research in the last month. I don't like what I see. What do you know about teenage alcoholism?"

Leslie wanted to deny any knowledge. But pieces of magazine articles and books leaped from her memory, drawing a picture that looked alarmingly like her younger brother.

Dad didn't force her to verbalize her thoughts. "Granted, we've only seen him drunk twice. But his behavior patterns are alarming. We can't afford to cripple ourselves with denial."

Leslie still couldn't look at him. She knew he spoke the truth, but it sounded too ugly to be real.

Dad lowered his voice to a gentler tone. "Leslie, see what's happened to us since Saturday. We should be enjoying Vince's visit. Instead, each of us has been locked away alone. We're hurting, but we usually share our hurts. We're too afraid to acknowledge the pain because it means admitting the source. Les, look at me." He waited for her to comply. "I haven't told you often how much I've appreciated your support with Mum and your help with Andrew over the years. But I need you more than ever right now. The pain of honesty will be easier if we share it."

The appeal in his eyes crumpled her resistance. She reached out her arms for a hug as she had when much younger.

Leslie felt her tears soaking Dad's shirt as they clung to each other. Waves of emotion left her shaken. First, the heartache she'd been trying to avoid for two days. Then the relief of knowing she needn't carry the hurt alone.

A familiar note of teasing shaded Dad's voice above her head, though he still spoke softly. "Are you getting salt stains on my shirt?"

She pulled back to smile wetly at him, only to see moisture on his cheeks, as well. "Probably no more than you got on my good sweat suit." She watched him wipe his eyes with his thumb, and marvelled at his willingness to cry. "Thanks for being you, Dad."

He squeezed her shoulder. "You're okay, too."

"Mind if I join the mutual admiration society?"

Leslie looked around Dad's arm to see Vince filling her doorway. "Sure, if you think two oversized men won't overload the occupancy limit of my room."

Dad looked at Leslie carefully for a moment, then at Vince. He moved toward the hall. "Better yet, I'll get out of the way. Mum said something earlier about wanting to take a walk. You okay, son?"

"Fine." Vince shrugged. The stricken look Leslie saw in his eyes last night had hardened into something different. He stepped aside for Dad then joined Leslie on the window seat. After a moment, he looked at her with a forced smile.

"We haven't had a good talk since I came home. Tell me about this boyfriend or friend or whatever."

Leslie stared at the floor, wondering whether to open the subject. She felt fairly certain he hadn't come here to talk about Dylan, and wished he'd tell her what really bothered him. However, just having him here restored a sense of stability to her world. "For starters, he's about six foot three, thirty-one years old, dark hair, green eyes and a terrific sense of humor. He's a pastoral studies student in Dad's homiletics and theology classes."

"A reedy, bespectacled type?"

Leslie laughed. "Definitely not reedy. He used to be a roughneck before he started Bible School and still works on the rigs in the summer."

"Spectacles?"

"As if it mattered, no."

"I'm just being a pest. What has you worried?"

"I don't know how to explain it. I guess it's just that from our first meeting he's hung around. This week he vanished. I see him at a distance at school, but that's all."

"You sure you're just friends?" Vince's eyes held no teasing, just simple concern.

"Vince, I don't have time for romance right now!" Leslie spoke more sharply than she intended.

"What's time consuming about it?"

"Hours on the phone, going on dates, spending hours talking to each other, not to mention the possibility of it becoming permanent. The last thing this family needs is me running off and getting married."

"You're right. But if you had a proper wedding here in town, I think everyone would be delighted." The roguish grin appeared again.

"You know that's not what I mean!"

Vince quickly rearranged his expression. "Please don't get uptight with me for saying this, but it sounds like you're fussing because Dylan isn't doing the things you say you don't have time for."

"I don't want him to fall in love with me. I just want to know why he's suddenly disappeared."

"He's the only one who can answer that. Why don't you ask him?"

"I don't want to sound like a clinging female."

"I don't know him, but if your attempt to restore your friendship puts him off, is he the right kind of guy?"

The conversation had gone as far as Leslie wanted. "Is this really what you came up here to talk about?" She searched his eyes looking for a clue.

Something violent flamed in his gaze for a moment before he leaned forward to rest his head on his hands with his elbows propped on his knees. "Guess you were right, Little Sister."

"About what, Vinny?"

"The kid." He packed the words with venom.

"What do you mean?" She felt too exhausted to discuss the subject again, but didn't know what else to say.

"He's got a problem all right. I'd call it Bad Attitude, with capital letters."

"I'm sorry he blasted you last night."

"I don't care what he thinks is bothering him. He has no right to go around making the rest of us feel like heels for occupying the same house! What does he expect us to do, bronze his high-tops?"

"Vince, he was drunk. He didn't know what he was saying!"

"He knew all right. He just had to get drunk to find the courage to say it. Have you noticed the way he's treated me since I came home? Barely polite. I don't care what his problem is. He has no right to inflict it on me!"

Leslie felt an uncharacteristic urge to slap him, but

reminded herself this weekend was Vince's first exposure to what she'd been learning to live with. "Do you understand now what I meant about there being something seriously wrong with him?"

"There's nothing so seriously wrong an old-fashioned whipping won't cure it!"

"Karen reached the same conclusion." Leslie couldn't help the chill that crept into her voice. She felt like she addressed a stranger wearing Vince's face.

"Don't get miffed, Les." A ghost of Vince's charming grin flitted across his lips. "You're just overprotective. It's always been one of your most appealing traits."

"Don't you think Dad has enough experience with children to discern what kind of discipline Andrew needs?"

"Andrew's the *baby*, Leslie. Youngest children in families across North America have traditionally received the light end of family discipline. Parents get soft after so many years of child rearing."

Amazement at his introverted perspective silenced Leslie. She had no energy or desire to argue with him. Nor did she want to listen further to his opinions. "What would you like for lunch?" She tried to laugh.

"Ever the diplomat." Vince's voice held a trace of sarcasm, which hurt worse than his earlier tirade. "How about those grilled sandwiches you make with the canned beans and tomatoes and cheese? Unless, of course, Andrew might object."

"Vince, that's enough!" As usual, her control snapped suddenly. "None of us like Andrew's behavior any better than you do. But I don't see Dad acting like it's a personal affront. Go ahead and mope if you want. I'll call you when lunch is ready." She stalked out of the bedroom.

Andrew appeared in the kitchen as Leslie served Vince a second portion. "Hi, Les. Is there enough for me?" He looked at Leslie sheepishly.

She started to greet him cheerily, but Vince interrupted. "Sure your sensitive stomach can handle beans this early in the day?"

Andrew blushed and he turned to leave. "Aw, never mind, Les. I'll make a sandwich later."

Leslie grabbed the shoulder of his sweatshirt. "There's plenty here. At least take a plate of food with you." She glared at Vince. Usually he kept his charm so firmly in place, rudeness never showed through.

Vince maintained a steady glare at Andrew while Leslie quickly filled a plate. He didn't speak until Andrew reached the stairs. "If you're ashamed to eat with me, why don't you just apologize?"

Leslie saw Andrew hesitate. "Never mind, buddy." She tried to keep her voice steady and calming.

"He doesn't need to hide behind you, Leslie." Vince's voice became nastier. "If he's man enough to get sloppy drunk, he's man enough to explain his actions."

Timidity vanished from Andrew's eyes, replaced by a strange cunning. He set his plate down in front of Vince. "Part of winning a game is celebrating with friends. I don't suppose you would know beer is a common beverage at parties."

"And which incredibly stupid parent buys it? Or hadn't you realized drinking is illegal at your age?"

"Not in a private residence, or didn't your university professor teach you that?"

Leslie sensed the childish bickering covered more serious animosity. She wanted desperately to head off the confrontation. But how?

"I don't need a university professor to teach me how to behave," Vince snapped. "Too bad you haven't developed that skill."

"Just because you're perfect doesn't mean I have to be." Andrew's tone dropped from baiting to cold fury.

"All I want is a little decency, maybe even some respect for our family values."

"No, Vince, what you want is for me to be just like you." Andrew held Vince speechless with his gaze. "I've never been good enough for you, the one who's out to rescue the pitiful teens of Canada. You'll never get near them. They won't let you, with your pious, lofty attitude. I'm not perfect and I don't want to be if it means being like you."

Vince leaped to his feet and grabbed for Andrew who ducked. "I don't care what you think of me, smart mouth, just like you don't care what the community thinks of this family. Have you considered what you're doing to our testimony with your drunken rebelliousness? I'm not surprised Dad had to resign from the Board."

"You don't care about the family, either. You're mad at me because I don't idolize you. You're scared I'm going to ruin your precious Christian image. Know what? That's all it is—just image. At least I'm not pretending to be something I'm not." Andrew picked up his plate and turned toward the stairs.

"Wait just a minute!" Vince lunged again but a kitchen chair blocked him.

Andrew set the plate back on the table, but didn't back away. "Yes?" His raised eyebrows communicated infinite disdain.

"Don't look at me like some helpless child!" Vince's

hands clenched and unclenched but remained at his sides. "What do you mean pretending? I am what I am. You may not like it, but I'm not a hypocrite. I love our family. I won't let anyone or anything, including you, create havoc. If I were a phony, the church would have found out long ago. Or have you forgotten I was on the Youth Executive for five years, three of them as President? I served as Missions Youth representative, taught Sunday School, sang in the choir, and did a lot of things you've never tried."

"How could we forget the achievements of Mr. Super-Christian?" Andrew quietly walked up the stairs, leaving his plate behind.

Vince opened his mouth to reply, but the sound of a closing bedroom door stopped him. He looked at Leslie. "How can he just walk out like that?"

Leslie couldn't reply. Stunned by her brothers' anger, she knew Vince wouldn't tolerate hearing her new-found partial agreement with Andrew's accusations. She left the kitchen quietly, wishing she could talk with Dylan.

eleven

Curled in her window seat Wednesday evening, Leslie tried to concentrate on the novel she'd been reading intermittently for a couple of weeks. Dad had given her the book for Christmas, a story of a pastor struggling against unseen enemies. Ordinarily, the tension would have held her interest. Tonight, scraps of conversation from the past few days kept intruding on her make-believe world.

Vince's attitude had become increasingly intolerable. He had closeted himself in his room until yesterday afternoon when he left without explanation. Leslie waited up for him to return, but he only greeted her with a curt "You can go to bed now" and disappeared into his room again. At least he had shown up for breakfast this morning. She hadn't know whether to laugh or scream at his carefully worded explanation.

"I've decided to go back to school today, rather than on the weekend." Vince kept his gaze on the butter knife he stroked across his toast. "It seems Andrew feels threatened by my presence. It will be easier for you to deal with the situation if I weren't here complicating things."

Dad hadn't been fooled. "I appreciate your consideration, but it really isn't necessary. I'm sure you've studied the principle that healing only comes through honest confrontation."

"Yeah, well, I really need to get back early. I've got a

project due the first of next month." No longer the suave charmer, Vince acted frantic to get away. He had his car packed by noon and departed after bestowing perfunctory hugs on Dad, Mum, and Leslie. Andrew stayed upstairs.

"Leslie, telephone!" Dad's call brought a welcome interruption.

"I missed you at prayer meetin' tonight, luv." Granny's tone emphasized the sincerity of her words. "Ye be feelin' a'right?"

Leslie knew better than to hide from her friend. "Not exactly. We've had a rough weekend."

"I thought as much Sunday. Would you care to share dinner wi' me tomarra eve?"

"I'd love to!" Just the thought lifted Leslie's battered heart.

"That's grond! I'll send my other special guest to pick ye up, then, aboot five."

"I can drive myself over, Granny."

"I know ye can. Humor an old friend, will ye?"

"Sure. Thanks so much."

Leslie didn't think until after she hung up to inquire as to the identity of the other guest. Probably another older friend from the senior's complex. And Thursday was Dad's night to cook supper, too. Good. Her absence wouldn't inconvenience anyone.

She spent Thursday going over recent class notes. Strange how much easier she found studying when Dylan helped. *It's good for you to get back to doing things on your own,* she admonished herself.

"Hey, Les. Got something for you!" Andrew's voice held an almost forgotten enthusiasm.

"Come in." She turned from her desk as he entered

carrying a white rectangular box. "What's that?"

"Wilson's Flowers just delivered it. It's addressed to you." His eyes sparkled. "Who's it from?"

She lifted the lid slowly, a strange exhilaration making it hard for her to breathe. A single yellow rose nestled among delicate ferns, tied together with loops of yellow ribbon. Unfamiliar writing on the card instructed, "We'd be pleased if you would wear this tonight." No signature.

"I would guess it's from Granny Maxwell, since she's invited me for dinner."

"Oh. Boring." Andrew proclaimed. "I thought it was from someone exciting."

"James would never be this extravagant," Leslie teased.

"He'd have sent you one of those silk jobs, if he even thought of flowers. I meant somebody like that Dylan guy that's been hanging around."

"Would you put this in the refrigerator for me, please?" She turned back to her books.

Andrew paused by her door, then left.

Leslie's mind refused to return to Old Testament dates and locations. If the corsage were from Granny, she would have signed the card. Who else would have sent it? No matter how she reasoned, hope insisted Dylan might be present tonight. But he was supposed to be in Bayfield for the break. And after he'd avoided her last week. . .To her relief, the clock showed 3:30. Time to get ready.

She showered and washed her hair, mentally reviewing her closet contents. She had planned to dress casually, but the corsage altered things. Forty-five minutes later, she viewed her image in the mirror with approval. Careful attention to her hair had enhanced its natural curls. The shorter area around her face had responded better than usual to the curling iron and now looked softly attractive. Her black jumpsuit emphasized both her unusual hair color and the yellow rose, as well as making her figure look almost classy. Black high-heeled sandals and boldly styled black and yellow earrings made her feel completely ready. Well, almost completely. She glanced toward her window. If only she knew . . . .Was that the Princess coming to a stop by their driveway? Her thumping heart caused her hands to shake as she reached for her black patent purse. She watched him slam the car door then pause, looking toward the house. He bowed his head briefly before moving toward the front door. Should she hurry downstairs so no one else would answer his knock or would that seem too eager?

Dad's pleased greeting from downstairs indicated she had hesitated too long. She heard him coming upstairs.

"You look wonderful, honey. Did you see who's come to pick you up?" The corners of his eyes crinkled like they always did when he felt especially pleased.

"Yes. I thought he'd gone to Bayfield." Her voice came out squeaky.

"Just relax, Les." He put his hands on her shoulders. "Trust Dylan, all right? He's not the kind of guy to play around with your feelings."

"Thanks, Dad." She squeezed one of his hands gratefully.

"Go down and wow him." He followed her down the stairs.

Dylan stood in the entry, staring out the window in the door. He whirled around when Leslie's heel tapped the linoleum. "Hi, Leslie."

"You're my chauffeur?" She hoped she didn't sound

insulting.

"By orders of Granny Maxwell. Sure you trust me with this stunning woman, Dr. Carlson?"

Dad's gaze locked onto Leslie's. "Absolutely. Have fun, you two."

They rode in silence to the seniors' complex. Leslie felt a million questions, but couldn't find words for any of them. Once inside Granny's apartment, Leslie gazed around with delight.

The table had been elegantly set for three. Under soft lighting, fine white china sat on a mint-green tablecloth. Matching candles had been lit in the middle of the table; a peach and mint-flowered cloth doily lay under the candlesticks. Peach-colored carbonated beverages filled crystal stemware and crisp salads rested on small plates nearby.

"Like it, do ye?" Granny said, grinning like a child.

"It's wonderful!" Leslie hugged the older woman.

"Don't thank me. 'Twas all Dylan's idea."

Something both unsettling and reassuring glowed from his eyes, stopping her words of thanks.

Granny seemed to sense the tension. "Let's sit." She bustled to the kitchen then returned to the table with plates full of lasagne, garlic toast, corn and steamed broccoli. Dylan seated her, then asked the blessing.

Granny and Dylan chattered through most of the meal. The atmosphere remained light, yet gently quiet. When they'd finished, Granny pushed her chair back. "While I do dishes, I'd like you two to make yourselves comfortable in the living room. I'll bring dessert in a while."

Panic twisted Leslie's middle. "Are you sure you don't want help?"

"Perrrfectly cerrrrtin, luv."

Leslie obediently moved to the living room, settling nervously into the big, stuffed chair. To her surprise, Dylan moved the footstool in front of her and sat on it.

"Leslie," he whispered, then stopped.

She looked at him, strangely comforted by his uncertainty. Her direct gaze seemed to strengthen something hesitating in his eyes.

He cleared his throat. "Tonight's dinner was to apologize for not being a very good friend lately. This," he gestured toward the rose, "is to tell you I don't intend to let it happen again."

Leslie didn't know how to reply, but she didn't look away from his face.

"I want you to know what I've been thinking."

"You don't—"

"Yes, I do." He interrupted her gently and reached out to hold her hand. "Since I want you to trust me, I have to be transparently honest with you. Our skating excursion started me thinking. You probably don't remember what James said, but some of his comments hurt. I had to sort out why I wanted your friendship. I realized if someone like James could drive me away, I'm not much of a friend. But I've also been thinking about the future of our friendship and wondering if I'm really the kind of friend you need. I finally talked with Granny Sunday evening and she helped me be more objective."

"I wish you'd told me what you felt." Leslie wanted to ask what conclusions he'd reached.

"I wanted to, believe me. But I didn't want to scare you with my uncertainties. I'm sorry I didn't let you know I wasn't upset at you."

"I wondered until Dad talked to me about the importance of trust. He said it makes the difference between acquaintances and friends."

Dylan sat silently, though Leslie could feel his hand trembling in hers. Finally he said so quietly she almost didn't hear, "Do you trust me, Leslie?"

Though uncertainty hovered in his gaze, she realized he would never deliberately hurt her. Her rioting emotions settled into tremulous confidence. "Yes."

He hesitated again, studying her face. "I know you're leery of emotional involvement, but I've realized this week I love you." He took a deep breath and rushed on before she could reply. "I'm not asking you to respond now. I'm just asking you to trust me enough to let me love you."

Leslie couldn't answer. Dylan's words kindled a spark of joy that wrestled against her burden of concern about Vince and Andrew. How could she make a decision about love while her family struggled? "I don't know what to say."

A gentle touch on her shoulder made her jump. "Dinna mean to startle ye, luv. Ready for banana cream pie?"

Dylan looked up at Granny, the apprehension draining from his face. "Two pieces, here, please."

A giggle bubbled from Leslie, taking some of her tension with it. "Just one for me."

Granny brought the pie, and chose a seat on the couch across from them. "You mentioned the weekend had been rough. Want to tell us about it?"

With a sense of relief, Leslie let the story pour out. When she finished her pie, Dylan took her plate and wrapped his hands around hers, all without interrupting.

She checked his eyes often for signs of boredom or rejection. Instead, gradually intensifying affection threatened to short-circuit her thoughts. "I never thought Vince would be so intolerant," she finished.

Dylan moved to let Granny sit on the footstool, but he retained his gentle grip on Leslie's hand. Granny clasped her other one. "I've no doot this is hard, luv. But ye cain't make yersel' responsible for your brithers' actions."

"But they're making life harder for Mum and each other."

"Sometimes we jist hae to let those we love feel their own pain. Tryin' to protect them enables them to continue avoidin' reality."

Leslie studied the hands clasping hers, one pair white and wrinkled, the other tanned and strong. Could she really distance herself from her brothers' struggles?

"Let me tell ye, luv, what I see." Granny smiled lovingly into Leslie's eyes. "I see a beautiful young woman who wants wi' all her hairrt to do what's right for her family. I see the same young woman becoming a prisoner within herself. Sometimes I think Leslie is getting lost in the Carlson family."

Leslie felt like a spotlight had suddenly beamed into her heart, revealing its secrets. Dylan squeezed her hands. "We need to pray."

Listening to the prayers of these two friends soothed her. They uttered no condemnations of her brothers, only requests for peace and strength for her. Dylan's prayer brought tears to her eyes again and draped a comforting blanket of reassurance around her. She couldn't help but trust a man who knew and loved God so deeply.

twelve

Dylan hoisted the handle of Leslie's book bag over his shoulder and held the door open toward the main parking lot. "Just look at that sun! Methinks spring is on the way."

Leslie grinned. "That's what you're supposed to think. This country loves to get you keyed up for spring, then dump a foot of snow."

"Fine with me. That'll leave me more evenings in front of the fireplace with my favorite redhead."

As had happened frequently in the weeks since their dinner at Granny's, his affectionate gaze left her tongue-tied. She felt like she ought to respond in kind, but the words wouldn't come.

"So am I invited for supper?" Dylan inquired when the Princess finally rumbled to life.

"What if I say no?" At least her smile worked.

"Then I'll just ask your dad. Can we have chili casserole?"

She laughed. "Looks like you have my life all organized."

A sober expression flitted across his face. Leslie thought he muttered, "I wish" just before he glanced her way with a wink. "What are friends for? Tell you what, I'll even make the salad."

Leslie didn't bother changing her clothes before hurrying into the kitchen; all her work clothes needed washing. She also wanted to correct the mess she knew waited. A couple of weeks ago Andrew started having trouble getting up on time. The first morning, he'd stopped Leslie on her way down the stairs to ask her to make his lunch, "just this once and please don't tell Dad." He looked ill, and Leslie felt torn between his request and Dad's ultimatum. Dad walked in on her preparation and immediately ordered Andrew downstairs to do the job himself. The sight of food seemed to nauseate him, but Leslie knew better than to interfere. Since then, Dad made certain Andrew ate breakfast with the family to ensure he had plenty of time to make his lunch. Leslie tried not to notice his obvious discomfort and puffy face. She also said nothing about the mess which greeted her most afternoons. Today an open mustard jar sat next to the sink, lettuce leaves cluttered the floor beside the refrigerator, and cutlery smeared with a variety of condiments lay scattered across the counter.

"Hope nobody was hurt in this wreck," Dylan commented from behind her.

"Teenagers are incredibly resilient." Leslie tried to keep her voice light.

"Andrew must be in charge of lunch duty."

Leslie only nodded.

Dylan turned her to face him. "What is it? Something's bugging you besides the mess."

Before she could answer, Dad's voice greeted them from the entry. "There's a heap of yellow metal in the driveway that indicates I'm going to have competition for the leftover oatmeal cake."

She turned away from Dylan, whispering, "Not now." Forcing cheerfulness into her tone, she raised her voice. "Your student has not only invited himself for supper, but he's told me he wants chili casserole." She started cleaning up frantically.

The teasing disappeared from his voice when Dad spoke again, this time from directly behind Dylan. "What is it, Les? The high pitch of your voice tells me — whoa, stop right there. Excuse me, Dylan." Dylan stepped aside so Dad had a full view of the kitchen. "Is this the first time this has happened, Leslie?"

She shook her head.

"Why didn't you say something?" His voice held no reproach.

She shrugged. "It didn't seem important after the struggle we've been having in the morning. I hoped it wouldn't happen again."

"Honey, nothing about Andrew is going to get better if we just hope it will go away. Has he been doing his other chores?"

"No." Leslie looked from the floor to Dylan's empathy-lined face.

"I'm sorry I haven't checked up on him earlier. May I go upstairs and take a look?"

Leslie could only shrug.

Dad reached toward her. "Les, you're not on trial here. I wish you'd told me, but I think I understand why you didn't. Now that I know, I intend to keep much closer watch on things. If you want to clean up the kitchen, go ahead. However, I can do it when I come back downstairs."

She simply nodded as he let her go. When she opened the refrigerator to put the mustard away, a package of lunchmeat lay open on the top shelf and a mutilated tomato had dripped all over the bottom.

Dylan put his hand on her arm. "May I do this? You can

go upstairs for a rest while your dad and I make supper. You look beat."

"I feel beat," she admitted softly, still staring into the fridge. "It's obvious Andrew's getting worse. What do I *do*?"

Dylan pulled her into an embrace and pushed the refrigerator door shut. "That's your dad's job. Yours is getting ready for finals and keeping me out of trouble."

Leslie returned his hug. "Sounds like full-time employment. I'm sorry you have to get involved in our family mess."

He pushed away so he could look into her eyes, but gripped her upper arms firmly. "I'm involved because I want to be. I love you, and want to make this easier. I'd eliminate it if I could." He hugged her again.

Leslie let herself lean against him, soaking up the feeling of being protected. She kept one arm around Dylan as she turned to face Dad when he came into the kitchen.

"How long has it been since your laundry hamper's been emptied?" He looked puzzled.

"Awhile. I just haven't had time to get to laundry." She'd forgotten about the overflow of dirty clothes in the bathroom.

"I thought Mum volunteered to do it." His puzzlement deepened into distress. "Ours has been getting done. I assumed yours would be, too."

"Maybe that's all she feels she can do." Leslie wanted desperately to reassure him.

"In other words, you're back to doing practically everything."

"No. You've been keeping up with the dishes and helping with meals."

"That's not the point, Leslie." He shook his head and his shoulders slumped. "You're not solely responsible for us, despite what conditions indicate." He looked away from her. "What can I do, Dylan?"

Leslie also looked at her friend, wondering what he would say. Mum's voice from down the hall broke the silence. "Dan?"

"In the kitchen, honey."

Leslie watched Dad straighten his shoulders and try to banish his frustration before Mum saw him. He leaned down to give Mum a kiss. "Have a good nap?"

She smiled brightly at him. "The laundry this morning wore me out. I came in to make lunch and the disaster was more than I could face. Sorry to have left it for you." She directed her final comment at Leslie.

"Joanne," Dad said gently. "Why didn't you tell me you were having trouble with laundry?"

Mum looked puzzled. "Keeping your shirts clean and ironed has been all I could do. Since Leslie didn't complain, I guessed she was handling it all right."

"You've done such a good job raising her she doesn't complain about anything, even when she should. Do you feel up to going out for dinner?"

Mum's face lit up. "A date? Of course. I'll go brush my hair."

Dad rubbed his forehead and looked at Dylan and Leslie. "I guess that means you two are on your own. Sorry about the un-invitation, kids."

Dylan chuckled softly. "She needs you, Dr. Carlson. With your permission, I can take care of the workaholic."

For the first time since coming home, Dad smiled. "I don't know what we would have done without you, son."

Dylan watched Dad walk down the hall with heavy steps. "I think their 'date' will lift his spirits." He turned back to Leslie. "There's something about spending time with your best friend . . . ."

Leslie just smiled, her emotions too turbulent for words. She reached for the lettuce on the floor, but Dylan gently slapped her hand.

"None of that. You're going to relax however you want. When I'm finished here, we'll order in something. You want Chinese food, chicken, or pizza?"

"You know I can't refuse Hawaiian pizza."

Even the sight of the littered bathroom couldn't eliminate the delightful bubble in Leslie. What would she do when Dylan graduated and left Nipson at the end of the school year? She pushed the thought aside and stuffed towels and sweat pants into the hamper. Don't get too attached, she reminded herself sternly. Daydreams have to give way to family responsibilities.

Whistling from the kitchen banished the blanket of gloom creeping up on her. Regardless of what would happen later, Dylan was here now. And, oops, he'd heard her coming down the stairs.

"How do you expect to rest with a basket of dirty clothes in your arms?" Affection in his eyes gentled the reproof.

"I have to do it, Dylan. I don't have a clean pair of pants left. And no, you can't do this for me," she added when he reached for the hamper.

"Stubbornness, thy name is woman," he muttered, but moved his hand from the basket to brush the hair away from her face.

The tenderness of his fingers on her cheek stirred her emotions afresh.

"Do whatever you need to do with that, and then rest, ok?" His thumb brushed gently across her cheekbone. "Those smudges under your eyes bother me." He dropped his hand to her shoulder and gave her a gentle shove.

"No need to get pushy," she retorted, then grinned, wanting to retain those moments yet uncertain of how to respond. She could feel his gaze follow her down the hall to the laundry room. When she came out again, soft humming drifted from the kitchen.

She left her bedroom door open slightly so she could hear the humming while she rested, or rather, daydreamed. How could those wonderful green eyes read her emotions so accurately? What in his personality made her feel ready to explode with emotion, yet unable to say a word? Snuggled under a comforter, she closed her eyes, remembering their conversations, the walks they'd taken, and the jokes they'd shared.

She woke to find her room much darker than she remembered. Now the humming came from somewhere in the hallway.

"Dylan?"

"Right here." He pushed her door open a little further.

"What time is it?"

"Around seven. Ready for supper?"

"Seven? Did I fall asleep?"

"Near as I could tell, and with the neatest smile."

She sat up quickly to cover her confusion. "What about the pizza?"

"Relax." One quick stride brought him beside her, where he folded himself into a sitting position on the floor. "I came up to check on you after I finished dishes, and decided to wait to order the pizza until you woke up."

"Aren't you starved?"

"Quit worrying." He enfolded her hands in his own. "If I'd been that hungry, I could have found some leftovers in the refrigerator, which, by the way, is now clean enough for military inspection. Come take a look." He stood and pulled her up beside him for a long hug. "You're pretty special, you know that?"

As they walked hand in hand toward the stairs, Leslie noticed one of the texts from Dad's theology class on the floor by her room. "How did that get here?"

A light blush crept up Dylan's neck. "I decided to study while you slept."

"On the floor beside my room? What's wrong with the dining room table or Dad's study? I'm sure he wouldn't have minded."

"That wasn't where I wanted to be," he said quietly, before gesturing grandly around the kitchen. "Does this earn your approval, madam?"

"It hasn't looked this good in months."

"So that means I get anchovies on my pizza?"

"On your half if I get pineapple on mine."

In what seemed like record time, their food arrived. He sent her to the family room, where he had lit the logs in the fireplace. Feeling relaxed and a little reckless, she positioned the beanbag chairs as close as possible facing the fireplace. Dylan appeared with one of the fancy silver trays Leslie often used for family parties. "Looks good." He nodded at the seats and set the tray on the floor. Wedges of pizza reposed on good china; Pepsi bubbled in crystal goblets. A small candle sported a flame made from construction paper.

"Is that any way to greet my attempt to treat you to fine

dining?" Dylan tried to look hurt at her laughter, but his twinkling eyes spoiled the effect.

"But pizza on china? And that goofy flame!" Leslie chuckled again.

He grinned. "I thought you needed comic relief."

Amazingly, she found the words she sought. She kept her gaze away from his face so she wouldn't lose her nerve. "Your sense of humor has been an incredible gift. I'm glad God has let you hang around."

"Thanks," Dylan said huskily. "Your eyes often tell me how you feel, but it's nice to hear you say it." Moisture shimmered in his eyes.

The appreciation in his voice made her want to say more. "You've been so incredibly wonderful—" She nibbled at her pizza before her fear slipped out.

"What's at the end of that sentence?"

"You always manage to do and say the perfect thing to turn my life right side up after something like this afternoon. I often wish I could do something in return, but I never know what. I've never had a friend like you." She swallowed hard and decided to tell him what she'd been dreading all afternoon. "I don't know when and how our problems with Andrew will be over. You'd only be normal if you tired of the unending crisis. Besides, graduation is less than a month away. You'll be leaving Nipson for good."

Dylan gently took her empty plate, setting it on the tray. He turned so he could grasp both her hands. "Look at me while I talk, Leslie. I wish I had solutions for you and your family. I don't. I know this much: no crisis is going to drive me away from you."

"But Andrew keeps getting worse." She forced herself

to continue meeting his gaze.

Though he never broke eye contact, his eyes told her that for a few moments he focused his attention elsewhere. "I have a story to tell you. I've deliberately not told you before, but I think tonight is the right time." He moved the tray to the coffee table, then moved his bean bag even closer. He slouched down so his legs stretched out in front of him and reached an arm behind Leslie. "Go ahead and lean against me. It's going to be a long one."

Leslie moved uncertainly, wanting to be close yet afraid of her response to the physical contact.

Dylan waited quietly until she had settled against his shoulder, then curled his arm around her in a comforting hug. His free hand reached for one of hers. "Perfect."

She moved her head so she could watch his face.

"I have a sister four years younger than I, whom I haven't mentioned before, because I've learned to be careful where she's concerned. Just before her fourteenth birthday, the school board transferred students from our neighborhood to a new school. We didn't anticipate a problem. She had always been outgoing. She's a beautiful girl, musically and athletically talented. She makes friends wherever she goes. Especially with the guys." He chuckled softly and stared into the fire. Leslie let him remember in silence.

"We knew she tended to be insecure, but we didn't realize how much until this change. Overnight, she became obsessed with her appearance. When she went on a diet, we thought it was just a fad and would pass when she settled in. Not until she passed out during a basketball practise did we realize she had a serious problem. The first doctor told us she tended toward anorexia, but not to worry about her unless she lost another 20 pounds. She promptly lost the weight. Mother and Dad spent the next eighteen months taking Jenine from one clinic to another, trying to find help. The clinics did as much as they could, but she refused to admit anything was wrong. Instead she exercised like a maniac, spent hours alone in her room, and ate as little as possible."

The pain etched on his face twisted Leslie's heart. She held his hand with both of hers and waited.

"The helplessness was the worst. First I'd get angry at myself for being unable to do anything, then at Jenine for creating the problem. Meals became nightmares. Jenine pushed her food around on her plate and ate almost nothing. Mother ate thirds and fourths as if the extra food she ate would keep Jenine alive. My brother, Steve, grumbled non-stop about why didn't we ever eat anything decent. Dad ate in silence, often leaving the table after only a couple of bites.

"The week after I graduated Jenine ended up in the hospital again. This time they told us she probably wouldn't come out alive due to heart damage. She improved just enough to be taken off the critical list, but not enough to leave the hospital. I arrived home early from work one day to overhear Dad talking to our pastor. I'll never forget his tone as he said, 'I've decided God really doesn't care. I might as well be dead for all the use I am in finding a solution for my wife and daughter. Some days it's all I can do to keep from driving into oncoming traffic.'" Dylan pulled his hand away long enough to wipe his eyes.

He looked down at Leslie with a small smile. "That's when I left home." He stared into the fire again.

After minutes of silence, Leslie felt compelled to bring him back to the present. "Is she okay now?"

Dylan shrugged. "She's married and living about 75 miles south of Bayfield. I've had to accept that she may never be well."

"What about your parents?"

"It's been tough. Pastor Terry finally helped them acknowledge Jenine's problem really was *her* problem. It's taken several years for them to sort through their questions about God. It's easy in times of intense struggle to view God as an abstract rather than a personal, loving Father. But they've come through well, and have even started an Overcomers Anonymous group for parents of children with obsessive/compulsive behavior."

"Wow." Leslie didn't know whether she should ask the next question. She looked straight into his eyes, which slowly regained their sparkle. "Obsessive/compulsive behavior—is that like alcoholism?"

He nodded. "It describes any condition in which a behavior controls a person rather than the other way around. The behavior may be anything—dieting, eating, drinking, bathing."

She sat up straight with a painful thought. "Can responsibility be obsessive/compulsive?"

He nodded again, this time saying nothing. The love in his eyes cushioned her while she reached her own conclusions.

"That's why Dad has been so determined to lighten my work load. I thought he just wanted to be nice." She wished she could hide from the revelation. She looked away from him.

"Leslie." Dylan's voice deepened with more tenderness

than she'd ever heard. "When something goes astray in a family, everyone is affected. Your mum has been ill for a long time, and now Andrew has problems. Your response has been perfectly normal. I tried for the longest time to keep Mother from eating so much, to cheer Dad up, to talk Steve into better behavior, to bolster Jenine's self-confidence so she wouldn't diet. Instead, I drove myself crazy and ended up running away. Your mum and Andrew have to make their own choices, just like my family did."

"But Andrew's making the wrong ones!"

"So did Jenine. She still is."

"You mean Andrew might never get over this?" Her eyes overflowed at the thought.

He gently wiped her cheeks. "That's a possibility you have to face. That's why you can't afford to make yourself responsible for his or your mum's behavior." He pulled his handkerchief from his pocket, then hugged her tightly.

When she could speak again, she laughed shakily. "Do you realize how many times I've cried all over your shirt and used up your handkerchief?"

He smiled down at her. "Do I look like someone who minds?"

"I guess not. Just pray that I find my way through this confusion."

"I've prayed for you every day since you sprawled in front of me."

The jangling phone interrupted. Leslie glanced at her watch and hurried to answer. 9:00. Who would be calling at this hour? She picked up the receiver. "Hello?"

"Les, you've got to come." Andrew sounded hysterical. "We're here by ourselves and Tom's hurt real bad. I tried to get them to take us, but they wouldn't. You've got to help us! Hurry, Leslie!"

She forced herself to stay calm. "Where are you?"

"Carp Lake. Ken's cabin. Hurry. He's bleeding bad. I can't get him to open his eyes."

Leslie hung up quickly and turned to find Dylan beside her. "It's Andrew. There's terrible trouble."

thirteen

Dylan held Leslie's coat for her, then grabbed his own with one hand and her hand with the other. "It's okay, hon. We'll get there as quickly as I can."

Thankfully, the Princess started on the first try. "Where are we going?" Dylan asked.

"Carp Lake."

"That's a good fifteen minutes out."

"I know. He said something about Ken's cabin. I hope we can find it."

"Who's Ken?"

"I wish I knew."

Dylan reached across the seat to take her hand again. "Remember he made the choice, honey."

Leslie tried to put a smile into her voice since darkness obscured her face. "Thanks. I'm just scared of what I'm going to find."

"Whatever it is, I'll be with you." He squeezed her hand gently. "Shall we pray while we drive?"

"If you can pray with your eyes open." She tried to laugh. "I don't think I could come up with anything coherent."

"God knows. Father, we ask for your wisdom for whatever lies ahead and for your peace for Leslie."

Leslie waited for him to finish, but he remained silent. Finally she asked, "No amen?"

"I'm not finished praying. I just don't have words for

what I want to tell Him." Dylan's quiet confidence calmed her.

"You and God are close friends, aren't you?"

"Only He's better than a friend, because he knows me better than I know myself."

"I haven't been thinking of Him like that recently."

"I know what you mean." Dylan chuckled softly. "When life gets turbulent, it's easy to forget the One who's running it all."

"Have you figured out how Jenine's problem fit into God's plan?"

"No."

"Doesn't that bother you?"

"Only if I let it. If I could explain God, He wouldn't be God anymore. He would be a creation of my imagination. Scripture tells us He controls all things and He loves me with an everlasting love. Therefore, everything that happens to me fits within those parameters. I don't always see how it fits, but I have to rely on what He's told me about Himself and know everything's perfectly clear to Him."

Leslie pondered the concept. "That's pretty profound. How did you figure it out?"

"It's called survival. When I hit bottom out on the rigs, I had to listen for God's perspective or lose my mind. Ask Ken Smith how close I was. When I gave up trying to explain God and started listening for what He wanted to say, He gave me what I call the gift of faith." He paused.

"I'm listening," she urged.

"Just wanted to make sure you didn't feel preached at."

"No." She searched for the right words. "I think you're throwing me a life ring."

"Granny Maxwell explained it to me like this—faith is

actually unshakable confidence in the integrity of God's character. In other words, no matter what, I know God will act according to His character, which is perfect. Sometimes I can't reconcile what I see in my circumstances with what I know His character to be, but He's told me how He is, and I choose to believe it."

Dylan's words caused a fog of guilt around Leslie to thin. "I've felt like I had to justify what He's allowed to happen before I could trust Him."

He squeezed her hand again reassuringly. "Nothing bothers us humans more than lack of control. So we try to control the disasters that come our way. When we recognize who God is, we realize the control for which we seek is His management of our lives."

"You could say faith is the antidote to both enabling and obsessive/compulsive behavior." She could barely believe the peace enveloping her.

"I like your way with words, Les." He turned the car to the right onto a snow-covered gravel road. The headlights illuminated a number of tire tracks through the snow.

They rode in silence, Leslie once more wondering what they would find at this unfamiliar place. Dylan slowed the car as they approached a Y in the road. "Do you see any tire tracks on your side?"

Leslie peered into the darkness. "I don't think so."

"Then maybe the trouble spot won't be hard to find. Perhaps Andrew's buddies are the only ones to have been out here since the last snowfall."

"We can hope," Leslie muttered.

Lights glowed through the windows of a cabin off to the right ahead of them. No tire tracks were visible beyond the driveway. Dylan had barely stopped the car before Leslie leaped out.

The cabin door flew open before she could call Andrew's name. Andrew ran toward her. "Thank God you're here." He threw his arms around her and clung, sobs shaking his skinny body.

Leslie held him close, letting him cry his terror out. She saw Dylan enter the cabin and knew Tom would be taken care of. "Want to tell me about it?"

Andrew sobbed a couple more times. "Tom and Ken got into a fight. Ken threw a bottle at him. It smashed on his head. He started bleeding everywhere and they took off. I begged them to take us with them, but they wouldn't listen. Tom's gonna die and it's Ken's fault." He started shaking again.

Leslie just hugged him tighter. "We'll do the best we can, Andy." The nickname which he allowed only her to use seemed to calm him.

Dylan appeared in the doorway, walking as quickly as possible with Tom in his arms. The expression on his face looked carved in place. "Leslie, will you open the back door? We need to get this guy to town quickly."

She pushed Andrew away from her gently. "Andy, go turn off the lights while we put Tom in the car."

Tom's long-legged form occupied the entire back seat, so the other three crowded in front. Without maneuvering on her part, Leslie found herself between Dylan and Andrew. Much as she knew Andrew needed her comfort, she needed Dylan beside her. They drove in silence, with only an occasional sob or fragmented comment from Andrew.

Once on the highway, Dylan accelerated. "If the R.C.M.P. try to stop us for speeding, we'll just ask for escort to the hospital," he explained.

The mention of police shattered Andrew's slowly returning control. "Are they gonna be at the hospital? They're gonna think I killed him!"

Leslie tried to calm him, but his voice grew louder and more hysterical.

"Andrew, shut up!"

Both Leslie and Andrew jumped. Leslie looked at Dylan, flabbergasted by his uncharacteristic harshness. But Andrew's babbling stopped.

"How about if you tell me what happened—every detail." Dylan's voice held undeniable authority.

Andrew repeated the story he'd given Leslie.

Dylan pushed for more. "How many of you were there?"

"I dunno. Six or eight."

"What were you doing?"

"Just having fun."

"What kind of fun that got Tom and Ken into a fight?"

"Tom said something and Ken got mad."

"Were you drinking?"

Andrew lapsed into sullen silence.

"I agree. Stupid question," Dylan commented. "The stench of beer in that cabin almost scrambled my head. How are you going to explain half a dozen minors boozing it up?"

"We were just having fun!" Leslie couldn't believe the fury in Andrew's voice. "Don't start on me. I didn't hurt Tom. Ken did."

"I suppose you think if you jumped off a cliff, it wouldn't be your fault for breaking your neck." Leslie felt the tension in Dylan's arm as he gripped the steering wheel.

"If you're trying to lay a guilt trip on me, I'm not taking it," Andrew shouted. "What was I supposed to do? Stick my head in front of Tom's when Ken threw the bottle?"

"That might have been an improvement," Dylan answered with chilly calm.

"I don't have to put up with this!"

"And your sister doesn't have to put up with your leaving the kitchen in a wreck. Your dad doesn't have to put up with your sneaking around getting drunk however and whenever you can. Your mom doesn't have to put up with your sullen behavior breaking her heart. But you know something, Mister? They do it. Don't ask me why because I'd like to snap your selfish little neck. They just keep putting up with you. They're hoping and praying you'll come to your senses."

Leslie felt caught between two packages of dynamite ready to explode. She heard Dylan's anger mounting and knew Andrew wouldn't sit quietly much longer. "Dylan." She spoke softly but insistently. "Tom still needs help quickly."

Dylan sucked in an enormous breath, but said nothing. Leslie laid a trembling hand on his arm, which he acknowledged with a glance. Andrew muttered furiously.

Thankfully, Nipson streets were almost empty of traffic. Dylan screeched to a stop in front of the hospital's Emergency Room doors. He lifted Tom gently from the back seat. "Leslie, would you open the doors for me?" Only white tenseness around his mouth illuminated by the intense hospital lighting revealed his simmering anger.

Andrew shuffled into a seat beside Leslie in the waiting room. The hospital environment seemed to have drained his hostility. "D'you think Tom will be all right, Leelee?"

"The nurse said he's still breathing, so we can hope." She still felt torn between her brother and her friend. Dylan had been right about Andrew's selfishness. Yet her years of nurturing Andrew made her instinctively jump to his defense. Did a defense exist for him tonight? She'd better get in touch with Tom's parents.

Dylan found her returning from the phones. "You okay?" The angry glitter faded from his eyes.

"As okay as can be expected. I thought Tom's parents should be notified."

"Yeah. The doctor sent me out to make sure that had been done. I suppose Andrew didn't offer to do it." His voice hardened again.

"He's pretty shook up."

"I wish he'd get shook up enough to get his head on straight. I'd choke him if I thought it would do any good." His expression gentled and he brushed his hand down her cheek. "I'm sorry. I know I'm not helping."

She squeezed his hand. "You're here and that's enough."

He chose a seat on her left, which again placed her between him and Andrew as the doctor approached. Dr. Keenan cleared his throat and looked sternly at Andrew. "Your friend is very lucky, young man."

Leslie thought Andrew might explode again, but he looked at the doctor with a meek, "Yes, sir."

"You fellows had no business drinking. You know that, don't you?"

"Yes, sir."

"Your friend has a concussion and lost a lot of blood from a nasty cut. It could have been much worse. I suggest both of you reconsider your form of entertainment." The doctor turned to Tom's parents, who had just arrived, cutting off any reply Andrew might have made.

fourteen

Two weeks later, Vince and Andrew sat in opposite corners of the family room, where they'd been avoiding eye contact with each other for the past hour. Leslie, curled on a bean bag close to Dad's chair, felt trapped in nonverbal crossfire. During the assignment of chores, Dad had appeared cheerfully oblivious; however, his next words shattered the illusion. "Move into the family circle, boys. With Vince home for the summer, you're going to have to accept each other's existence. Let's talk about the problem before we end this meeting."

Andrew angled his long legs closer to Leslie. Vince had been moving in her direction, but he stopped and settled a short distance from his original position.

Dad spoke sharply. "Vince, I know Family Council isn't your idea of the perfect way to spend your first Sunday home, and I know you're not thrilled with taking on family chores. However, we are a family unit. Could I have a little mature cooperation from you?"

Vince's eyes narrowed and he stood as if to leave. "Excuse me. Maybe I should have found a job in Bayfield."

"That's enough." Dad hadn't increased his volume, but each of his words carried an authoritative punch. "It's time we reach an understanding."

Leslie held her breath, waiting for Vince's next move. She couldn't remember having seen this side of his personality before. He paused, then slowly settled on a nearby stool.

Dad's voice now seemed to reach across the room with empathy. "Why is the issue of family chores upsetting you so much?"

"Dad, don't you see how Andrew's problems are rearranging the whole family? During the last six months I've watched the family life I love disintegrate as a result of his irresponsibility, and you've done absolutely nothing. If I'd tried to act like that when I was his age, you'd have disciplined me quickly and sharply."

"Do you feel I disciplined you too harshly?"

"Of course not. I just can't help but wonder why you've been so lax with Andrew."

Dad inhaled deeply before answering. "Mum and I have never claimed to be perfect parents, but we tried to do our best for each of you. Our primary goal has been to raise you as the individuals you are. If we didn't treat you all alike, it's because you're not identical."

"Come on, Dad. You can't deny that Andrew's blown it big. When are you going to do something about it?"

"If I felt you were genuinely concerned about Andrew's welfare, I might answer that question. Instead, I suggest you pry into your own motives and actions. Meeting dismissed." Dad stood wearily and helped Mum to her feet.

Vince watched them leave, a mixture of anger and disbelief rippling through his expression. He shook his head at Leslie a couple of times, then left without a word. The front door slammed.

Leslie felt like she'd sat through a blizzard. Though the wind of Vince's fury seemed to have died, a chill permeated the house. "Lord, we don't need this," she thought, remaining curled on the beanbag. The confrontation had left her feeling stunned, hurt, and apprehensive. Slowly she became aware of someone else in the room and glanced toward the doorway.

The chuckle she loved lifted much of the gloom. Dylan remained leaning against the door jamb for another moment, then walked toward her, arms outstretched. "I wondered how long it would take you to realize I was here."

She could feel her smile responding to the sparkle in his eyes. "I didn't hear you at the door!"

"I came in as Vince was leaving. He looked like he might have something to do with the pain I've been watching on your face for the last few minutes."

"My hero's been acting like the selfish child he thinks Andrew is."

"If you're looking for a new hero, I'm available." He wrapped his arms around her.

Leslie returned the embrace, then looked into his eyes with her hands clasped lightly behind him. "I'd rather keep you as a friend."

"And do you greet all your friends like this?" Though his eyes twinkled with humor, he seemed to be searching for something.

"Just the special ones." She hugged him again quickly, then took his hand as she pulled away. "Since you're here, it must be almost time for church."

"Only if you feel up to going."

"Do I have enough time to change clothes? I left my watch upstairs."

"You look terrific as is, but you do have time. I came a little early. You've gotten me so addicted to your smile

I just couldn't stay away."

Leslie felt the blush warming her face. "I'll be right back." She scampered toward the stairs.

She grabbed a denim skirt off the hanger and her peach-colored sweater from the shelf. A pearl barrette, pearly earrings and a quick squirt of perfume, and she snatched her watch off the nightstand on her way out of her room.

"Do you have a curfew tonight?" Dylan helped her into her coat.

"No. Why?"

"I thought we might take a drive after church."

"Sure." Being with him always seemed to turn her family's problems into mirages rather than overwhelming substance.

Tonight's service was the Assembly's monthly "Worship Fest," in which various musical individuals and groups participated in two hours of special presentations. The music seeped into Leslie's spirit, bringing peace. Granny sat with Leslie and Dylan, often patting Leslie's hand after an especially meaningful song. When they stood to leave, she winked at Leslie. "Love looks good on ye." She chuckled and bustled off.

Love. Leslie felt the flush creep up her face while she pondered the word. Was that what she felt for her big, gentle friend? Or did she just enjoy being the focus of his attention? A glance at his face told her how he felt. How far should she let it go?

"Leslie, look at me," Dylan commanded softly.

Embarrassed by what he might read on her face, she reluctantly faced him.

"You don't have to be ashamed of loving me. I love you, too." He draped his arm over her shoulders and steered her toward the door.

She studied the sincerity in his eyes before she spoke. "But what if I don't love you?" As soon as she heard the words, she realized how they sounded. "I mean, you're the best friend I've ever had, but —"

"I know what you meant." He helped her into the car. "I'm not worried by your uncertainty, so you shouldn't be, either. Remember I told you once that when the time is right, the questions will answer themselves? It worked for me." His smile bordered on smugness, though the teasing twinkle in his eyes marred the effect.

"I just have so many questions!" She hoped her soft laugh would cover the desperation creeping up on her.

"Hey, don't panic. I'll wait as long as necessary. How about if you tell me about them. Even if I can't help, I'd like to listen."

"I'm feeling confused," she managed to say after a long pause. "Or maybe afraid. Even though I love having you around, I'm not sure I love you the way I should. And if I do, is this the right time? It seems like no matter what conclusion I reach, I find more questions."

"One of the many things I love about you is that doing what's right is important to you. But maybe you're making this more complicated than it is."

"What do you mean?" Leslie wasn't sure whether to be angry at him for not understanding or grateful for the relief he offered.

"Do you have any doubts about being with me right now?"

"No."

"Does our friendship as it is bother you?"

"No."

"Is it making life more difficult for your family? or for you in relation to your family?"

"No. In fact, Dad has mentioned several times how grateful he is that you help me keep my sanity."

"So it would seem most of your questions have to do with the future, right?"

She said nothing, embarrassed by his perception.

"Les, would you move over closer to me?" His right arm tugged on her sleeve compellingly, then settled around her shoulders when she slid to the middle of the seat. "There's nothing wrong with having questions about the future. But there are some things we just have to leave with our Heavenly Father. Can you do that with us?"

"But what if I don't love you? What if I'm just using your affection to distract me from the mess at home?"

Dylan said nothing until they came to a crossroad where he could pull off the main highway and stop. "Let's get out and walk for a bit. Leslie, who is going to get hurt if you discover you've just been using me?"

She felt grateful for the darkness that had fallen while they drove. "You will and that's what I'm afraid of."

"But I've already considered the options, and I'm not worried about it."

"You mean you don't care if I hurt you?"

"I didn't say I don't care. I meant I'm willing to take the risk."

"But why?" The words fell out of her mouth before she could stop them.

"Because I love you, and because I feel our friendship was designed by our Father. Since we both want only His best, I'm willing to wait as long as it takes for love to develop."

"And if it doesn't?"

"I'll grieve, but I'll also rest in knowing He's the God Who does all things well. If this isn't His best for us, I'm willing to experience the pain necessary to find His best."

Something in Leslie twisted sharply at the idea of a different relationship being best for either of them, but she remained silent. If she didn't love him rightly, she had to be willing to let him find love elsewhere.

Dylan spoke again, his voice barely above a whisper. "Honey, can you just let me love you and let God take care of the future? Hey, look up there."

Over their heads, glowing patches of green, yellow, blue, pink, and purple danced around and through each other. "I've never seen Northern Lights so vivid before." She matched his quiet tone.

"Listen."

She stood as quietly as she could, trying not to breathe. Through the silence that enveloped them, she heard a faint tinkling, like faraway bells. "What is it?"

"I call it the music of the lights." He moved behind her so he could hug her without blocking her view. "You only hear it when the lights are really bright, which is usually on nights when there's no moonlight."

They stood for several moments watching the fantastic display above. Then Dylan turned her to face him in the faint light. "Love can be your music while you're coping with the midnight your family's in right now. Will you let it?"

She wrapped her arms around him, soaking up his affection. "I just don't want to take advantage of your love if I can't return it."

"You return it in many ways you're not aware of yet."

He gently tipped her head so he could look into her eyes.

"Really?" Leslie felt so captivated by the open love in his face she didn't realize what had happened until his lips gently touched hers.

"It seems I love you more each minute I spend with you, Leslie-love. Your eyes tell me my case isn't totally hopeless."

For the first time, Leslie knew it, too. His tender kiss had silenced the tumult, leaving only a gentle awareness that somewhere in the recent past she'd given her heart away to the best possible caretaker.

fifteen

"What's with him?" Dad asked, noticing Dylan waiting on the steps when they arrived at school Monday morning. Uncertain eagerness and attempted nonchalance mingled on Dylan's face.

"Who knows?" Leslie tried to restrain the joyful giggle which bubbled in her throat. She hurried to greet him. Something on her face must have reassured him, because his uncertain expression vanished in a face-splitting grin.

"I wasn't sure you'd still be speaking to me after my performance last night." He sounded concerned. "I wouldn't change a thing, but I thought I might have scared you off."

Joyful certainty filled her again. "Not a chance."

As each day passed, Dylan found new expressions for his affection. He left goofy notes in her textbooks, causing her to choke on laughter in the middle of a class. Each time the end-of-class bell rang, she found him waiting in the hall. Rather than being frightened, Leslie felt released to discover the depths of joy his love revealed in her. He took her home from school each evening, stayed for supper, and didn't leave until late. Though Leslie could tell from the twinkle in Dad's eyes he'd noticed the change, to her relief, he said nothing. She still didn't feel ready for explanations.

The other three members of the family seemed oblivious. What little time Vince spent at home, he hid in his room. Mum seemed more troubled than usual, though Leslie often discovered her washing dishes or vacuuming. Andrew alternated between fun-loving helpfulness and silent sullenness. Just thinking of the varied family climate dimmed her exhilaration as she walked home Thursday afternoon. Maybe she should have waited for Dylan to finish his test so she wouldn't have had to come home alone.

"Don't be a baby," she instructed herself. "Their moods don't have to mess up your life."

Thirty minutes later she didn't feel so sure. Breakfast dishes still filled the sink along with last night's supper dishes, which Vince had mumbled about taking care of this morning. A quick glance at the downstairs bathroom revealed an accumulating mess, and upstairs the laundry hamper overflowed. She felt no desire to cover up Vince's neglect. His attitude toward Andrew since spring break had been completely different from anything she'd ever seen in him. Her anger sparked. Why couldn't he see how his self-righteousness made life difficult for the whole family? He acted like only he was affected by Andrew's problems!

For once, Andrew's door stood open, so she paused in the doorway. "How's it going, buddy?"

"Just great," he replied cheerily, quickly turning his back so Leslie couldn't see what he held.

"Doin' anything tonight?" She felt compelled to continue the conversation.

"Uh, yeah, I mean no, I mean—" His voice trailed off and his neck and ears grew red.

"Hey, I'm not trying to rope you into anything. I just like to know what my family's doing."

"It's nuthin' bad, I promise." He still refused to look at her.

Apprehension formed a cold puddle in Leslie's middle. She didn't want to pry, but if she could talk him out of something foolish, she had to try. "Let me guess. You've decided to cook supper for me."

He turned to grin sheepishly at her. "Good guess, but wrong. Besides, Vince wouldn't eat it."

"Don't fret about him, Andy. You're not responsible for his attitude."

"Yeah. He still makes me feel like scum. That's why I decided to be absent tonight." He spoke with a burst of feeling, then looked startled at what he'd revealed.

"I wish you wouldn't, buddy."

"Les, I've been grounded for the past month. Most of my friends have forgotten I exist. This is the first time Tom has been well enough for a party since Ken beat him up. I've got to go!"

She wanted to ask about adult supervision and alcoholic drinks, but knew both subjects would arouse hostility.

He seemed to read her mind. "Don't worry. Tom's parents will be there and you know they don't allow drinking."

"Then why don't you just ask Dad?"

"I can't, Les, and that's all there is to it. It's perfectly harmless and as long as Dad doesn't find out, nothing will happen. Just forget I said anything, ok?"

"Sure." Walking to her room, Leslie felt completely dispirited. She dumped her bag beside her desk and changed from her green and rust plaid skirt and green pullover to jeans and a yellow sweatshirt. Her hamper overflowed with laundry, but she didn't feel right about doing hers without Andrew's too, and that would leave a fraction of the job for Vince. She had enough clean clothes to last for awhile, at least until Dad got after Vince. The ringing doorbell interrupted her planning.

When she opened the front door, she gasped with surprise at the flowers being offered by a deliveryman. He grinned at her reaction, but merely said, "I hope you're Leslie Carlson?"

She nodded and took the delivery from him. A small card in an envelope pinned to the plastic film confirmed her hopes. "To my friend and sweetheart. Hope this will brighten your day in my absence. All my love. D." She carefully set the arrangement on the table so she could remove the plastic. Two roses nestled in a cloud of baby's breath in a simple crystal vase. Though she knew her family would enjoy seeing the flowers, their message was too personal for general observation. She carried them up to her desk. Her whole room seemed suddenly brighter. She sat on her bed to drink in the beauty of the flowers and the love they communicated. Maybe Dylan would be finished with his test by now so she could thank him. He answered the dorm phone on the second ring.

Leslie laughed. "Were you waiting by the phone?"

"Should I have been?" Affectionate humor rippled through his tone.

"Someone sent me two gorgeous red roses, and the card attached had a wonderful message in your handwriting. If it wasn't from you, someone's trying to replace you. I'm partial to flowery gestures and mushy messages."

"Now that's a switch. You're pretty wonderful yourself." The tenderness in his voice reached through the telephone and wrapped itself around her heart.

"Thanks. I'd like to hug you for that."

"I'll settle for a kiss next time I see you."

"Hmm. Maybe." She pretended to consider. "Are you coming over tonight?"

He chuckled. "I wish I could. Does that count?"

"Perhaps. You'll have to wait and see."

"And maybe I'll have to have a talk with your dad. By the way, how are things at home this afternoon?"

"I'm not sure."

"Sounds serious." His voice dropped its playfulness.

"It's Andrew. He's planning to sneak out tonight to go to a friend's birthday party. He's only three days away from having his grounding lifted, and I don't want him to ruin it."

"But that's his decision, honey."

"I know. Should Dad know what's up? Or should I leave well enough alone, and let Dad discover on his own?"

"That's a tough one. All I can do is keep praying for all of you." He paused. "And remind you that no matter what, I love you."

"I love you, too, and wish I could have told you something besides more bad news."

"What are friends for? Besides, it's not that bad yet."

"Thanks. I guess I'd better let you get back to the books."

"Your call has improved what was going to be a long, dreary evening. And sweetheart?" He waited for her to answer.

"Yes?"

"If you need to talk to me for any reason, even if it's early in the morning, promise you'll call."

"You asked for it." She laughed uncertainly.

"I mean it. And don't forget you're loved."

She hung up the phone, wondering how much of the conversation Andrew had heard. She looked up the stairs at the familiar closed door. The question of whether or not to tell Dad rumbled back and forth through her thoughts while she thawed meat and peeled potatoes.

"I didn't hear you come home." Mum's surprised voice came from behind Leslie's post at the sink.

Leslie turned to smile at her. "I've been here for a little while. How're you feeling?"

"Pretty good." The brightness of Mum's eyes confirmed her words. "What's for supper?"

"Hamburgers and homemade fries. Dad has a late staff meeting, and I thought this could be kept warm easily. Besides, it's one of Vince's favorites."

"Maybe Vince should cook his own dinner."

Leslie tried not to show her surprise. "Why do you say that?"

"He's not helping like he should, and even I can see his attitude getting worse." Though she spoke sternly, Mum's face looked like she was commenting on the weather. "I've noticed the mess in the bathroom and the overflowing laundry hamper. Do you want to mention it to Dad or shall I?"

Leslie vocalized her first thought. "Whatever you think is best, Mum."

"Maybe I'll talk to him. Would I be able to make some dessert without being in your way?"

"No problem. I'll be mostly here beside the sink and the stove." Leslie felt like a stranger had taken over Mum's body.

They worked together, mostly in companionable silence, though periodically Mum asked questions about Leslie's classes and teachers. Vince came home at 6:30, but aside from a growled inquiry about supper, remained silently in his room. Andrew's door stayed shut.

When she heard Dad's car in the driveway, Leslie unobtrusively positioned herself where she could watch his reaction upon seeing the new bright-eyed, cheerful Mum. Though his eyes lit up and he grinned lovingly at Mum, his face registered little surprise. Leslie wondered if she'd missed something.

Vince and Andrew diligently avoided eye contact during supper. Vince helped himself to two hamburgers and a full plate of fries immediately after Dad finished the blessing. Andrew ate little. Mum and Dad carried the conversation, while Leslie kept serving dishes full and watched quietly.

Vince bolted his food then mumbled "Excuse me" and left the table. His bedroom door shut firmly. Leslie felt like a thundercloud had passed by. Andrew departed much more quietly.

Dad reached for another helping of fries. "Thanks for supper, Les. I imagine you have studying to do for upcoming finals?"

"I still have another week before testing starts," she explained. "Besides, most of my classes will have essay tests, which I find fairly easy."

"I'm just concerned, remembering the difficulties you had before spring break. Don't let us mess up finals for you."

"Not to worry. Do you have time for a chat later on?"

"Sure. I didn't bring any homework, so whenever is good for you."

Mum spoke up. "How about if I call Andrew to help me clear the table and do dishes. That way you two can talk now, and I'll have Dad to myself for the rest of the evening." She smiled teasingly at Dad.

"Sounds terrific to me," he responded. "Okay with you, Les?"

She nodded, stunned afresh by Mum's amazing change. How long would it last?

"Let's just be grateful she's feeling better," Dad said when she voiced her thoughts in his study. "Granted, it's been years since I've seen her this perky, but I've learned to simply thank our Father for her ups and let the downs take care of themselves. What has Andrew done to worry you today?"

Leslie couldn't hide her surprise. She'd wondered how to bring up the subject without feeling like a tattletale. "How did you guess?"

"You had your mother-hen look at supper while you watched him out of the corner of your eye. Besides, the worry lines between your eyes are different for each member of the family. When it's Dylan, the lines droop all the way down your face."

Leslie laughed. "Ok, I'm transparent. What can I say?"

"How about starting with your brother?"

"He told me he's planning to sneak out to Tom's birthday party tonight." She hesitantly related her conversation with Andrew, ending with her instincts about the evening. "It sounds stupid, but I'm worried that everything's not going to be as Andrew says. But what can happen with Tom's parents there?"

"It's not stupid. Remember the parental sixth sense I've told you about? I've learned over the years not to discount it regardless of how ridiculous it seems. It's why I introduced you to Dylan." His grin could have beat Dylan's best for mischief.

"I'm glad you did, though my memory of our meeting doesn't include you." The mention of her favorite subject melted the chill of worry.

"You never did tell me what happened the first time he brought you home."

"I told you my book bag dumped and I tripped over the contents."

"He's just been around so much since I thought there had to be much more to the story." His eyes still twinkled with mischief.

"Maybe Dylan can tell you more, but I can't."

"You'd be surprised at what he's told me."

"Oh really?" Leslie tried to look disapproving before she admitted, "Actually, your friendship with him was one of the reasons I liked him so much from the start. But that's beside the point. I still don't know what to do about Andrew."

"Do we really have to do anything?" Dad emphasized the last word.

"But what if he gets in trouble again?"

"Isn't that his responsibility? He knows he's breaking the rules and he's also old enough to know right from wrong. He may be lying to us, but he'll just have to suffer the consequences."

"He seems oblivious to his own problem."

"Self-deception gives addiction its power. Until he's honest with himself, he can't begin recovery."

"What if he gets hurt like Tom did?"

Dad sat silently for several moments, then moved to

stand beside Leslie with a hand on her shoulder. "Have you considered that Andrew's addiction may kill him?"

She felt a cold fist imbed itself in her stomach. She had tried not to think about the possibility. "It can't affect his health so drastically this early, can it?"

"You know there's more to it than that. Accidents involving alcohol are still one of the major threats to teenagers. They don't realize they're impaired and do things even more foolish than they would otherwise." He wrapped his arms around her. "It's a horrible thought, Les. Yet we have to accept Andrew's freedom to make his own choices. We can't protect him from himself. All we can do is continue to pray for God's protection. Shall we pray about it together?"

Leslie didn't realize how long they had talked until she passed the kitchen on her way upstairs. Both Mum and Andrew had finished clean-up, including the dishes Vince had left earlier in the day. No lights remained on in the dining room, living room, and kitchen. She wandered up the stairs, thinking about Andrew as well as prioritizing her study until the end of exams in two weeks. The rosey fragrance wafting from her room reminded her afresh of Dylan. She paused to appreciate the smell and to relish the feeling of being loved. A draft from down the hall interrupted her thoughts. She glanced toward the doorway of Andrew's room. Just beyond, a breeze from the open window flapped the curtains.

sixteen

The next day crawled by in a fog of exhaustion. Leslie slowly gathered her belongings after her last class, barely remembering what material had been covered.

As usual, Dylan hovered outside the classroom door. "You look beat, love."

"Yeah. I didn't sleep much last night."

"I just have to sign the graduation gown order form at the office and I'll meet you at the car. You'll be okay waiting for me?"

"Of course." She revelled in his worrying, especially after expending so much on her younger brother. It felt good to be taken care of. She envisioned Dylan in his graduation gown at the ceremonies just two weeks away. He hadn't mentioned where he planned to work afterward, but she hoped he could find a job nearby. A familiar tall figure striding across the parking lot halted her musing.

"Vince! What are you doing here?"

"I came to give you a ride home from school." His words sounded friendly, but his expression looked thunderous.

"Thanks, Vinny, but Dylan has already offered."

"That's great!" he exploded sarcastically. "I go to the effort of arranging my schedule to get here and you say no thanks. Why not tell Dylan no thanks?"

Leslie stood helplessly stunned by the tirade. "I'm sorry. . . ."

"Why do I always have to adjust to everyone else? Just

like what Dad calls 'family chores.' Since when is schooling such a drain you can't keep up with normal housekeeping? Why do I get saddled with the work? If you need help, Dad should get Andrew to take care of it. A little hard work might keep him out of trouble. But what does Dad do? Nothing. I'm sick of this whole mess and I wish just one person would take a look at my perspective—"

A familiar firm voice interrupted, "I think that's enough, Vince," while a comforting arm slid around Leslie's shoulders.

"What do you know, Bible School boy? Why don't you try living in the real world for awhile instead of complicating our lives from the fringes? Leslie's never been too busy for homemaking until you showed up."

"Vince, I said that's enough. If you need to vent your frustration on me, I'll be right back. First, I need to get your sister home for some rest."

"And why is that? Because of that irresponsible kid—"

"Never mind him, Leslie." Dylan steered her firmly toward the car and Vince's acid verbiage fell silent when he realized they weren't listening. "I hope he doesn't do this often."

"He's been building up to it ever since he came home," she admitted, "but he's never let it all out like this. He's ragged Andrew a couple of times about Andrew's 'Christian witness.' I wonder if he's aware of how badly he's blown his own. My family is becoming a crowd of strangers." She shook her head wearily.

Dylan helped her into the car and took her hand after settling on the driver's side. "Honey, you're too tired to make sense of it right now. Mind if I talk to your dad?"

"Sounds good." She felt relieved someone else wanted to take care of this newest complication.

A soft tapping at her bedroom door awoke her two hours later. "Leslie," Dad called softly. "Supper's ready."

She stumbled sleepily down the stairs to the table, where toasted bacon and tomato sandwiches sat at each person's place, along with steaming bowls of corn chowder. "Thanks to the cook," she mumbled, then realized only four places were set. "Where's Vince?"

"He's eating in his room. We'll talk about it later. I've called Family Council right after supper." Though his eyes looked grim, Dad smiled at her. "Let's eat, family."

Leslie tasted her chowder, marvelling at its fresh, creamy flavor. "What brand is this? I'd like to get it again."

Dad's eyes twinkled briefly. "Mum's brand. She's tonight's cook."

"You made this from scratch?" Leslie could hardly believe her ears. "I hope you'll let me in on the recipe—it's terrific."

"You were sleeping so soundly, I figured you needed the rest." Mum's face showed the same unusual alertness it had yesterday.

Leslie looked at Dad, wondering whether to comment on the change, but he shook his head slightly and winked. She took the cue and concentrated on her food.

Mum offered to wash the dishes, but Dad directed everyone to the family room immediately. He rapped sharply on Vince's door, then followed his son into the room.

"Boys, you might as well know you're the subject of discussion tonight. Andrew, your actions last night need explanation and Vince, your attitude needs changing. Andrew, let's start with you." Dad waited for Andrew to speak.

"It was just a birthday party, and I had to go so I went."

"But you had been grounded, which means you weren't supposed to go anywhere but school. And that still doesn't explain your condition when you did come home. You didn't act like it had been 'just a party'."

"We were at Tom's. His parents were there and nothin' happened. We had cake and pop, played games, and came home. That's all." Andrew's eyes developed defiant glints.

Dad said nothing while he watched Andrew patiently. The boy shifted in his seat, but also remained silent.

Finally, Vince broke the impasse. "It's obvious he's not going to talk, Dad, so why don't we get this meeting over with. I didn't see him last night, but even I can tell from his behavior now he was drunk. If you think he's going to admit that, you're more naive than I thought."

"Vincent, you will apologize to your Dad for your words as well as your tone. You may not agree with him, but he is still your Dad, and by Scripture, entitled to honor." Mum held Dad's hand tightly, but her voice carried more authority than Leslie had ever heard. Vince's arrogant expression dwindled into stubbornness. Mum continued. "I believe Scripture also says something about removing the big problems in your own life before you attack the little ones in another's. I would suggest an attitude adjustment on your part before you criticize your dad or anyone else." She stopped as though suddenly aware of her own words. She glanced at Dad uncertainly. "I didn't mean. . . ."

"That's just what we needed to hear," Dad reassured her.

Vince launched his self-defense again. "It appears that I'm the only one around here who has to change. I could point out areas of weakness in everyone here, but I'm the only —"

"Not only could you, but you have," Dad interrupted swiftly. "And I'm tired of it. Your constant sniping at Andrew is completely out of order. Have you studied addictions in your psychology courses? That's what your brother is fighting and he needs your support, not your criticism."

"Addiction?" Vince's face paled and Leslie thought she saw a glimmer of the older brother returning. "What do you...you mean he's an al...he's got a drinking problem?" He looked stunned.

"Yes, son, I do mean he's an alcoholic," Dad responded softly, his words laced with compassion.

Leslie looked at Andrew. Relief and denial struggled for control of his expression. He made no move to leave the room.

"But he's a Christian!" Vince's tone revealed his incredulity.

"How does that preclude his problem?" Dad watched Vince closely.

"Christians don't have addictions."

"I'm sorry to break this to you, but Christians are human." Humor twinkled out of Dad's eyes.

"That's not funny. You and Mum are Christians and worked hard to raise us all properly. How could Andrew let this happen?"

Dad smiled reassuringly at his youngest son before replying. "Vince, have you heard the saying 'Christians aren't perfect, just forgiven'?"

"Well yes, but we all lose our tempers occasionally or fail to witness when we should. But alcoholism!"

"Why do you think one kind of sin is more acceptable than another? Did Jesus teach a grading system for sin?"

"No, and alcoholism is sin, like murder. Losing my temper is a mistake."

"How about self-righteousness?" Dad let the question hang quietly.

"What do you mean?" Vince suddenly looked defensive.

"Or self-pity? Apparently quite a show of that, along with temper, took place in the Bible School parking lot this afternoon."

"And who told you that? Probably goody-two-shoes Stoddard, who thinks he's got some sort of claim on Leslie. He's getting as bad as Trindle."

Leslie wanted to jump to Dylan's defense, but Dad silenced her with a glance. "Dylan does have a claim on Leslie because he's decided to love her. That claim includes the responsibility of protecting her from unwarranted attacks."

For a moment, Vince looked like he'd been slapped, then arrogance swiftly covered his face. "That finalizes my decision. I've already talked to Karen and Brad and I'll be moving out there tomorrow."

Stunned silence filled the room after Vince stomped out. Leslie looked first at Andrew, whose face remained impassive, then at Mum.

"I'm okay." Mum smiled reassuringly.

Dad cleared his throat. "So Andrew, I guess we still haven't finished our discussion about last night. Are you ready to talk now your chief accuser is gone?"

Andrew stared at the floor for several moments. "It was nuthin'—" he began.

"Son." Dad's voice compelled Andrew to look up. "I've heard that explanation twice and it won't work. How about telling me what really happened."

"We're not drunks!" Sudden anger raised Andrew's voice.

"What's your definition of a drunk?" Dad let him ponder the question, then asked another. "Why was this party so important to you that you'd lie and sneak around to get to it?"

"I wanted to see how Tom is doing."

"You know you could have asked me to take you to visit him and I would have been glad to do so. Did you know someone would bring beer?"

Andrew nodded, then burst out, "But I'm not a drunk!"

"Then why do you drink?"

He considered. Leslie saw anguish in his eyes. "Dad, you don't know what it's like when the guys won't let you be part of the gang 'cause they think you think you're too good for them. After our first win in the fall, I drank a beer at the party just to show them. Now we do it to have fun."

"But it's illegal."

"Yeah, but we make sure we don't get caught. It's like a super-party, you know? Nobody's mad at anybody, you can tell stupid jokes and everybody laughs, and we're all just good buddies. It's fun."

"You used to have fun like that with the youth group."

"Yeah, but now I just feel stupid."

"Perhaps because you've forgotten how to have fun without being drunk?"

Andrew stared at the floor.

"Andrew, you're an alcoholic."

"I am not!" He leaped to his feet angrily. "I just like having a good time."

"Then I want you to relearn how to have a good time without the beer. You're not getting your driver's license back until you can prove to me alcohol is no longer part of your life."

"You just don't want me to have any friends except the ones you pick." Andrew's face reminded Leslie of Vince's expression less than an hour earlier.

"No, son, I love you too much to let you ruin your life, which is what these friends are encouraging you to do. You can invite them to the house if you like, but there will be no alcohol of any kind on this property. You're free to come and go as you please, provided your family responsibilities are taken care of. If you're not an alcoholic, then it shouldn't be a problem to tell your friends you won't drink with them until you're old enough to do it legally." Dad stood and squeezed Andrew's shoulder, then drew him into a hug. "I love you, son."

Mum joined them. "I love you, too."

Tears welled up in Andrew's eyes again, though Leslie saw desperation hovering behind his gaze. He pulled away from his parents only to put his arms around his sister.

"What's this about?" She tried to laugh, though the unexpectedness of the gesture choked her up.

"Thanks for puttin' up with me, Leelee," he replied. Three long-legged strides took him out the door.

Leslie felt too drained to move. Various facial expressions hung in her memory like a collection of snapshots—Mum's determination, Andrew's defensive desperation,

Vince's angry arrogance. "What's made Vince so angry at us?" She heard her voice crack and tears threatened to spill over. She swallowed them back for what seemed like the hundredth time since his scene at the Bible College.

"It's not us, Les." Pain laced Dad's voice. "Vince has just never had to cope with anything serious not going his way. He's angry at life, maybe even God, though he'd never admit it."

Mum rubbed his back gently. "His solutions to Andrew's problem are much like Karen's."

"Mm. That feels good." He relaxed under her ministrations, then chuckled softly. "The simplest answers are always most obvious from the outside. You know, in all our discussions, I don't think Dylan has ever offered a solution."

Leslie felt the affectionate smile spread across her face. "He's been in our shoes. He knows how useless easy answers are."

Dad slouched against the back of the couch with his legs stretched out in front of him. "Has he told you what he's planning to do when he graduates?"

"I don't think he knows yet. I hope it's nearby."

Dad reached out to smooth her hair. "I know it's easy to say, but don't fret about it too much, honey. Even if he has to leave Nipson, he'll keep in touch. Or maybe he'll take you with him."

Leslie looked straight at him, her eyes widening with surprise. "Not now!"

"I thought married couples did things as a team." His eyes twinkled mischievously.

"But we're not getting married—I mean not right away."

"So you've discussed it?"

"No. I just know it's not right at this time." She tried to sound more certain than she felt.

"And how do you know?" His hand moved from her hair to her shoulder.

"What if I don't love him enough to make marriage work?"

"I thought you were pretty fond of the big guy."

"I am."

Dad pulled her into a leaning position against his knees. "Books and movies have us convinced rampant emotion is the basis for marriage. Even though excitement may initially attract us to our marriage partner, only the decision to love makes the relationship last."

"But how do I know he's the right one?"

"That's a decision only you can make. Knowing you both as I do, I could tell you what I hope for, but I won't. I'll just tell you two things. First, keep praying about it. Your Heavenly Father is intimately concerned about your happiness and He'll help you decide. Secondly, I heard a Christian speaker say one time that it's time for two people to consider marriage when they are more effective together than they are separately. Maybe that would be a good concept for you to discuss with Dylan."

Mum spoke up. "Maybe some of what I've been thinking recently will help." Leslie turned to look at Mum in surprise, catching Dad's loving nod. "You've been wondering about me, haven't you?" This time Mum looked at Leslie, who also nodded, then leaned her shoulder against the couch so she could watch Mum's face.

Mum hesitated briefly. "Watching you this spring has reminded me of myself at your age and I've wondered where I'd lost my enthusiasm and the ability to cope which you've shown." She paused and studied hers and Dad's hands clasped in her lap. After a moment she continued.

"My illness after Andrew's birth left me emotionally drained. Gradually it became easier to stay depressed than make the effort to re-enter life. Your dad tried to help me, but I wouldn't let him. I learned to retreat from crises in a variety of ways.

"Our family meeting about chores a couple of months ago started me thinking about areas of my life I had abdicated to you and Dad. The morning Vince left after spring break, I realized I'd become absent from those I loved without leaving the house. I decided I would try participating in life again. I didn't want to make a big announcement because I didn't feel sure I could change. Vince's scene this afternoon showed me I can cope, especially with your Dad around." She sent him a love-filled smile.

"You did more than cope, Mum." Leslie squeezed Mum's hand affectionately. "Vince needed to hear what you told him."

"I wanted to give him the spanking of his life."

"He looked like he felt spanked." Dad chuckled. "He wasn't expecting opposition from you."

Mum looked back at Leslie. "We're getting off the subject. If you feel anything like I felt when your Dad first told me he loved me, you're wondering if you can live up to Dylan, right?"

Leslie felt stunned. Mum's perception clarified what had been vague apprehension. "Right," she managed to say.

"I've missed out on a lot over the years because I let

feelings of inadequacy put me in hiding."

After a few moments' consideration, Leslie asked, "What's the alternative?"

Dad answered this time. "Just be yourself. Neither of you ladies are aware of how special you are."

"But how did you know about each other?"

Mum looked at Dad for several moments before answering. "I'm still not sure. I guess I just decided to take the risk of letting myself love him, and I haven't regretted it. There's nothing more wonderful than being partner with a man who cherishes you with a love based in his love for God. When Dylan looks at you, I see in his eyes the same steady love your Dad has given me for almost thirty years. That's a treasure you can't afford to turn your back on."

seventeen

For the first few days after Vince moved out, life felt unbalanced. Though Mum spent a lot of time sleeping, she also managed to accomplish an amazing amount of housework, including laundry. Andrew kept up with his chores and maintained a relatively friendly demeanor around the family. But the look in his eyes bothered Leslie. Shadowed by desperation, they looked like the eyes of a trapped animal. When she tried to encourage confidences, he just smiled and assured her he felt fine. Karen still called every few days; she rarely mentioned Vince and Vince never asked to speak to anyone in his parents' house.

To her surprise, Leslie didn't feel bound by the worry that had dogged her earlier in the year. She felt a strange detachment from the whole family. Her feelings toward Dylan, however, were anything but detached. She snatched every possible minute to be with him. The more time they spent together, the more Leslie knew her feelings for him were genuine.

The few days before his graduation seemed idyllic. No longer afraid of her feelings, she felt carried through final exams on a glorious tide of exuberant affection. Only thoughts of Dylan's plans after graduation marred her joy. A lazy afternoon together in the park finally gave her a chance to voice her fears.

Dylan lay stretched out on a picnic bench, his tie loosened under his sweater and his shirt collar open. She sat on his jacket on the ground beside him. He half-opened his eyes to give her the special long look that made her feel like the only woman in the world. "Don't fret, Les. Regardless of where I have to go, my heart will be here in your busy little hands. I'll set aside a substantial budget for phone calls, and will probably get so lonely for you I'll have to write."

"A real honest-to-goodness letter? I thought real men didn't do letters." She tried to laugh.

"You never know what lengths of desperation I'll be driven to. But for now, let's just enjoy being together."

They spent the rest of the afternoon basking in the sunshine and talking. Dylan only let go of her hand periodically to give her shoulders an affectionate squeeze.

Finally Leslie looked at her watch, then gasped. "Dylan, I've got to get home! It's a quarter after six. Dad will already be there, and I haven't done a thing for supper."

"They can't cope by themselves?" he responded with a twinkle.

She couldn't help laughing. "That's not the point! I'll even invite you to stay, if you'll just take me home now."

"You didn't know I was planning to stay anyway." He gave her a gentle lingering kiss, then picked up her book bag. "Think we can get this to the car without something escaping?"

"I have full confidence in your extraordinary abilities."

He grabbed her hand again and pulled her into a run. They reached the car, laughing and breathless. "What's that?" She pointed to a folded piece of paper under his windshield wiper.

Dylan helped her into the car first, then walked around to check. He grinned like an excited small boy when he opened the driver's door. "Listen to this. 'Dylan and Les, Should you find this before 7 p.m. please meet us at the Ranchlands Dining Room. Dad and Mum.' I told you your dad would understand."

"I'm not really dressed for a fancy dinner." Leslie looked down at her grey cords and blue and grey flowered cotton sweater.

"I hadn't noticed, but if you want to improve on perfection, we'll stop by your house on the way."

Changing clothes only took minutes. She quickly took from the back of her closet a dress she'd been saving for a special occasion. Made from a mint green silky material, its full skirt reached almost to her ankles. Full sleeves fastened just below her elbow and she snapped a gold bracelet around her wrist. Cream nylons matched her cream high-heeled sandals that had sparkling gold buckles at her ankles. Dangling gold and rhinestone earrings sparkled through her hair, which she touched with a curling iron to make it fluff around her face. A quick spray of perfume and an application of lip gloss sent her back downstairs in just under fifteen minutes. "Ready to go, Dylan."

"Looking like that, I'd rather keep you to myself, but duty calls." As she slid her arms into the coat he held, he leaned forward to whisper in her ear, "I love you, beautiful."

This time her response came without forethought or struggle. "I love you, too."

"Should I have changed clothes?" He steered the car out of the driveway.

"I think I recently heard someone say you can't improve on perfection." She glanced approvingly at his black dress pants only slightly wrinkled from the day's wearing. He'd buttoned his white shirt collar and tightened his tie, which matched his forest-green sweater.

Just before entering the restaurant, he paused. "Are you sure we shouldn't ask for a table just for two? I don't want to waste a romantic evening like this."

"As long as you're willing to explain to Dad." She grinned.

But, they agreed later, the evening had been perfect even if they hadn't been alone. Dad and Dylan inspired each other's humor to increasing heights of goofy fun. Mum and Leslie alternately participated and laughed themselves breathless.

After dessert arrived, Dad took a deep breath and his face sobered. "Joanne and I want to thank you for sharing with us one of your last evenings together. Dylan, we also want to thank you for the help you've given Leslie during these past few months. She couldn't have had a better friend." An unspoken message passed between the men. "Wherever you have to go after graduation, I hope you'll remember you're always welcome in our home."

Dylan had to clear his throat a couple of times before speaking. "Thanks, Dr. Carlson. You, too, Mrs. Carlson." He seemed unable to go on. Moisture in his eyes surprised Leslie. He reached for her hand and swallowed hard. "Tonight will remain in my memory as one of the best ever." Again Leslie sensed communication between him and her dad she couldn't interpret. Mum smiled at them both like she harbored a delightful secret.

Dylan didn't take Leslie straight home. They drove around Nipson, remembering other drives and reminiscing over landmarks with special significance. Eventually they came to an intersection between the highway and a secondary road.

"Do you remember this, Les?" Dylan asked, parking the car at the side of the secondary road.

"You kissed me for the first time." She snuggled close to him, wishing she could see his face in the darkness.

He put his arm around her shoulders and held her tightly. "You were uncertain about something that night, and we agreed to let time take care of it. If I'm not mistaken, your question's been answered, hasn't it?"

She wondered how he'd guessed. "I think so."

"I'm glad. I've seen a lot more lately of the spontaneous, affectionate person I'm sure is the real Leslie."

She waited, unsure of where he was taking the conversation.

He cleared his throat. "Much as I'd like to ask you something here tonight, I'd rather wait until I get back from Bayfield." His voice trembled slightly. "The answer is so important to both of us I want you to have lots of time to think about it. That's part of why I'm staying in Bayfield for a week before looking for a job. I want to give you time and space to think. Do you understand what I mean?"

For a moment Leslie wondered if she'd ever breathe again. How many guys gave their sweethearts advance warning of a proposal? But then not many girls seemed to have her trouble interpreting their own hearts. She nodded against his shoulder, unable to say more than, "Thanks, Dylan." Their lips met in the dark in a kiss filled with promise.

Dylan pulled away with a shaky laugh. "Much more of that and your dad will accuse me of undue influence. Mind if we go home now?"

Tender silence lingered while they drove, until he asked softly, "You'll miss me?"

She pretended to think. "Probably. I'll miss you telling me what to fix for supper right after you've invited yourself, I'll miss having no leftovers, and getting phone calls when I'm trying to sleep in. Yeah, I guess I'll miss you."

"And I'm going to miss that funny choke of yours when you don't want to laugh. You won't forget how to laugh while I'm gone, will you?" He parked the car at the curb in front of the Carlson house and pulled Leslie into a hug. "I can do this now since I don't have to worry about messing up your hair. You looked gorgeous tonight, honey."

Leslie relaxed against him, relishing the solid security of his embrace. "I love your hugs," she murmured against his shoulder.

"You don't appreciate my kisses?"

She could visualize his raised eyebrow. "A kiss is exciting, but a hug feels more permanent, less like you're leaving soon."

He tightened his arms. "Like I said earlier, my body has to go to Bayfield, but I'm leaving my heart with you."

eighteen

Graduation Day dawned bright with sunshine, though Leslie felt like she moved in a fog. The ceremonies were impressive, and Dylan received a standing ovation for his valedictory speech. He made sure she met his parents, a friendly grey-haired couple.

Leslie felt a strange sense of relief at the instant rapport among her parents and Dylan's. Dad praised Dylan's scholastic abilities to Mr. Stoddard, who listened in beaming silence. Mrs. Stoddard and Mum compared notes on the food being served at the reception. Dylan and Leslie mingled with other students and parents, Dylan making sure Leslie never strayed far from him. Gradually, the crowd thinned.

"Dad wants to leave in about an hour," Dylan said unsteadily when they saw his parents approaching. "Do you want to help me pack and we can drop you off on our way out of town, or would you rather go home with your parents?"

Leslie blinked hard and tried to laugh. "I have this thing about watching people drive away. Do you mind if we say goodbye now?"

"Just a minute." He put one hand on her shoulder and motioned to his parents with the other. "I'll meet you guys up in the dorm in a few minutes." They caught his meaning and changed direction. He turned Leslie so he could look straight into her eyes. "This isn't goodbye, love, only see you later. I'll be back in a couple of weeks." He kissed her gently, then held her in a long, tight hug. "I'll call you tonight when we get in."

"I'll be waiting." She tried to smile, but tears filled her eyes. "I love you."

"I love you, too. Keep track of this for me, will you?" He pressed something into her hand, hugged her again quickly, and strode toward the dorm without looking back.

Leslie looked down at the clean handkerchief in her hand and felt the tears start in earnest. A comforting arm slid around her waist.

"Ready to go home?" Mum's soft voice inquired.

"Yeah." Leslie tried to grin.

Dad's arm went around her other shoulder. "Dylan warned us you might be feeling tearful, but told me to be sure to remind you he'll be back. He even told me to come after him with a shotgun if he hasn't shown up within two weeks."

Saturday and Sunday felt strangely quiet. Leslie missed the routine of classes and studying. Mum had done spring cleaning, leaving her little to do but think.

Church on Sunday morning helped a little, though Granny's hug made Leslie's tears start again. Granny just squeezed her hand compassionately and whispered, "He told me to remind you he'll be back as soon as he can."

Leslie shut herself in her bedroom as soon as they arrived home. A knock at her door thirty minutes later didn't surprise her.

"Need help thinking?" Dad's voice carried both laughter and empathy.

"Sure." She didn't move from where she lay across the bed staring at the ceiling.

He pulled her chair close to the bed and sat down. "Want to tell me what's bugging you, or shall I guess?"

"Since I don't know what I'm thinking, what's your guess?"

"You're wondering how to choose between Dylan and us."

The statement felt accurate but sounded totally wrong. "How do I avoid making a selfish decision?" She sat up slightly so she could watch Dad's face.

Dad's eyebrows approached his hairline. "Selfish?"

"What about Andrew and Mum?"

"What about them?" Dad's voice lowered ominously.

"What if they don't get better? Mum's made amazing progress, but who's to say how long it will last? And no one knows how long it will take Andrew to straighten out."

"You don't need to worry about us, Les." Dad's voice gentled. "What's happening for you is the way God arranged life's cycle. If you're taking the next step within His guidance, He'll make sure those you love are taken care of."

"But what if Dylan gets called to a church more than a few hours away from here?"

"Maybe that would be healthiest for your marriage." Dad's use of the word sent tingles down Leslie's spine. "Your Heavenly Father calls it 'leaving and cleaving.' We'd miss you for sure, but that's our challenge. Yours is to be the wife to Dylan God intends you to be."

Dylan's wife. Leslie hadn't thought in those specific words. Delightful images filled her imagination. Cooking for just the two of them. Decorating and taking care of their home. Being part of Dylan's life every day.

"Your face glows like you're getting the message. If you're as terrific a wife as you are a daughter, Dylan's one blessed man." His chuckle lingered after the door closed behind him.

Leslie lay back again, this time with pleasant thoughts. What would Dylan say if she said yes? What new expression would show up in his eyes?

She wasn't aware she had fallen asleep until an insistent ringing awakened her. Turning her head from side to side to loosen the cramped neck muscles, she wished the noise would go away. Through the thickening dusk, the sight of a police car in the driveway startled her to full alertness. She bolted down the stairs and dashed into the entry.

A short R.C.M.P. officer stood ramrod straight with his back to the door, turning his hat over and over in his hands. Dad looked at him, his face a pasty grey and his eyes shadowed.

"Dan, what is it?" Mum gasped from the doorway beside Leslie.

"Andrew. An accident at the gravel pits." He swallowed hard, unable to go on. One step took Mum to him, where they clung to each other.

"I'm sorry, ma'am." The officer cleared his throat. "He's still breathing, but it looks bad. We'll provide you with escort to the hospital. You may not have much time."

Leslie felt like the scene slowed to half speed. As though watching a movie, she saw her parents draw apart to reach for their coats. Though tears glistened in Mum's eyes, an unfamiliar strength seemed to be holding her upright. Dad shook his head a couple of times and a little color came back into his face.

"Leslie." His gentle voice recalled her to a reality she didn't want to face. "Are you coming?"

She opened her mouth to answer, but no words came. He handed her a coat. She followed him mutely. As she stepped outdoors, a piercing wail assaulted her. Lights flashed blindingly. Gradually, she realized the noise and light came from the police car parting traffic ahead of them.

A white-coated nurse came toward Dad and Mum as soon as they stepped through the emergency room doorway. "Mr. and Mrs. Carlson?"

Dad had regained his composure. "Yes, ma'am."

"The surgeon will be here in just a moment, but we need your signatures on these consent forms."

"Just show me where."

"Can we see him?" Mum sounded breathless.

The nurse smiled at them compassionately. "I'm sorry. He's already been prepped. He's been unconscious since he came in, so he wouldn't know you. We're going to do the best we can to make sure you can talk to him when we're finished."

Leslie heard what the nurse tried not to say. In spite of their best efforts, she might never hug her little brother again. The room tipped crazily around her. She leaned against a nearby wall, wishing it were Dylan.

"If you'll come this way," the nurse was saying. "There's a quiet room where you can wait. We'll let you know as soon as there's any kind of change."

Dad and Mum followed her, their arms tightly around each other. Leslie stumbled along behind. The room was comfortably small without being cramped. Pale blue carpet matched the upholstery on modern style wood-framed furniture.

The nurse gestured at a phone on the small table. "If you need to call anyone, dial 9 to get an outside line. A coffee machine is just around the corner." She gently clicked the door shut when she left.

Dad and Mum settled on the loveseat, and Leslie chose a chair close by.

"How are you doing, Les?" Dad looked closely at her.

She shrugged. "I won't know until they're finished."

"Did the officer say what happened?" Mum whispered.

"You heard it all." Dad sighed heavily. "I'm sure there was drinking involved."

Mum leaned her head on his shoulder and again Leslie wished for Dylan. After several moments, Dad reached for the phone. "We need to let Karen and Vince know."

Mum looked at her watch. "We should call the church, too. Service will be starting in less than a hour, so someone should be there."

"Good idea, hon." He dialed quickly.

Leslie leaned her head against the wall behind her and closed her eyes to try to shut everything out. "Lord, I need Dylan," she thought, not aware she was praying. Slowly the prayer became intentional. "Father, You've said You won't give us any more than we can bear. Please show me how to bear this. If Andrew should—" She couldn't even think the word, much less pray it. "Please don't let anything happen to him, Lord." Tears ran out from under closed eyelids and ran down her cheeks. She sat up and looked around her chair for a tissue box. To her surprise, she found her purse clutched in her lap. She couldn't remember having gone back to her room for it. She fished inside for tissue. Her fingers encountered a piece of cloth—Dylan's handkerchief. She buried her face in the large white square, letting sobs shake her.

Strong arms embraced her. "It's okay, Les," Dad whispered, while Mum gently stroked her hair and murmured comfortingly.

"What if—"

"That's not important now." Dad quickly interrupted. "The nurse said he's still breathing and his heart still seems strong. Let's not borrow trouble."

Mum laid her head on Leslie's shoulder, and Leslie could feel her tears soaking her sweater. Leslie moved one arm to embrace Mum and felt Dad embrace them both. She felt his tears dampening her hair. Finally, Dad straightened and reached for the tissue box nearby. "Let's pray. Heavenly Father, we all need You like we've not needed You before. Right now we have no hope and no strength but You. We don't understand why this happened, but please enable us to hear whatever You will speak. Father, please make your presence exceptionally real to our boy upstairs." His voice broke. Leslie felt a tremor go through him before he continued. "Guide the surgeon's hand and grant the entire surgical team great wisdom. Andrew is precious to us, Father—" His voice trembled, and Mum sobbed quietly. "—yet we know he's more precious to You. We trust You, Father, to do what's best."

Though he didn't say Amen, the three of them raised their heads at the same moment. "Thanks," Leslie and Mum said together, then smiled shakily at the coincidence.

A loud voice in the lobby broke the quietness. "Where's Andrew Carlson? We've got to see him. We're relatives."

Dad grinned a bit. "Brad," he said simply, and left the small room.

"Oh, hi, Dad. Is he out yet? How did it happen? How long will he have to stay in the hospital? Do we need to get him anything?" The barrage of booming questions grew louder.

The door opened. Karen released her grip on Brad's arm to fall weeping into Mum's arms. Brad continued to fire questions at Dad. A grim-faced Vince settled stiffly into the chair beside Leslie. "He was drinking again, wasn't he?" he whispered fiercely.

Only the pain in his eyes prevented Leslie from making a sharp retort. She clasped his hand. "We don't know yet, Vinny. They're just trying to keep him alive."

So the family waited together. Leslie didn't know whether her nap in the afternoon relieved her of the need to sleep or if worry kept her awake. Karen and Mum dozed leaning against their husbands, who took turns providing coffee and tea. Though Vince sat with his eyes closed, Leslie could tell from his stiff posture he wasn't sleeping.

After a couple of hours, someone knocked softly on the door. Karen let out a startled cry, then buried her face against Brad's chest. Mum's gaze simply followed Dad as he opened the door. The police officer who had come to the house stood in the doorway.

"May I come in? We've discovered some details I thought you'd like to know." He shook his head at the chair Brad pushed toward him. "As you probably guessed, a group of high schoolers were partying out at the gravel pits. The number of empty beer bottles in the area indicates they were drinking heavily. Someone had a three-wheel all terrain vehicle. They were taking turns riding. Your young man was the unlucky one who tried to take it up a bank that was far too steep. The ATV turned over backwards, landed on top of him, caught his foot under the seat, and dragged him down the hillside."

Karen sobbed with great gulping noises. Mum moaned softly, then covered her mouth with one hand. Dad moved to stand beside her, his arm around her shoulders.

"Sorry to be so graphic, ma'am, but there's no gentler way to say it." The officer's eyes revealed his dismay at being the bearer of gruesome details.

"It's all right, sir." Mum's voice trembled. "Please go on."

"There's not much else. Fortunately a couple of the kids were still sober enough to realize your boy was seriously hurt. They drove to a nearby gas station, called us and the ambulance." He shifted his weight slightly before continuing. "I hate to say it, but you seem to be the kind of folks who'd want to know. I'm sorry, sir, but your boy was one of the most severely inebriated."

Dad extended his hand toward the officer. "We guessed as much, sir, but thanks for coming." The two shook hands, then the officer lifted his hat in Mum's direction and left.

Vince sprang to his feet at the same instant Dad shut the door. "What was Andrew thinking?"

Dad cut him off with a hand on his shoulder. "Enough, Vince. Let's make this as easy for each other as possible, at least until we know what the prognosis is." His tone brooked no disagreement.

Vince subsided once more, leaning against the wall with eyes closed. Leslie felt the familiar emotional tearing, hating to see her elder brother so angry with the younger, yet loving both intensely.

"It's okay, Les," Dad whispered. He placed his hand reassuringly on her arm, then settled once again on the love seat beside Mum, drawing her against him.

Periodically, a white-clad figure entered briefly to tell them surgery was still in progress, Andrew was still "doing as well as can be expected" and the surgeon would come talk to them when he finished.

Somewhere close to midnight, Leslie sensed a change in the stiff, angry form beside her. She turned her head to see Vince slowly crumple with his head in his hands. Silent sobs convulsed him. She put her arm across his broad back, hoping he would accept her comfort. Glancing at Dad, she saw him gently ease Mum's sleeping form against a cushion before he moved to kneel in front of his son. He pulled Vince into an embrace.

Vince slowly gained enough control to speak. "I'm sorry, Dad. I can't stay angry at him when he may be dying."

Dad wisely said nothing, letting Vince's repentance flow without interruption. Eventually Vince lifted his head to look into Dad's eyes. "Will you forgive me for being so obnoxious to you?"

"Of course." Dad smiled more broadly than he'd done since the police had arrived six hours earlier.

Vince turned to Leslie. "I've been a real pain to you, too. Can you forgive me, sis?"

"What are sisters for?"

Vince's head dropped into his hands again. "I just hope he makes it so I can tell him how sorry I am," he whispered hoarsely.

"Son, we can't lose hope until there *is* no hope. Remember our Heavenly Father's in control of every detail." Dad's eyes looked a little brighter.

Leslie studied Mum's face, thinking of the incredible changes which had taken place in the last couple of weeks. Somehow, this crisis enhanced Mum's new-found strength. Leslie had half expected her to be devastated.

Her gazed moved to Brad and Karen, sleeping in each other's embrace. No major changes there, though she couldn't bring herself to be angry with her sister's emotional theatrics. A new perspective gripped her, enabling her to view her sister with detachment. Aggravating though Karen could be, Leslie realized she genuinely meant no harm. It was just her way of handling crises. Leslie wondered absently what arguments between Karen and Brad were like. She could mentally hear Brad booming and Karen shrieking and crying. She shifted in her chair and felt her back muscles cramp after hours of sitting tensely in one place.

The door opened gently to admit the nurse. "The doctor sent me to tell you that if your boy hangs on for another hour, he stands a good chance of making it. After that the surgeon will just have to do the final sutures and bandages." She smiled encouragingly at Dad and Leslie and backed out.

"He's hung on this long," Leslie whispered.

Dad nodded. "Thank God."

That last hour dragged on longer than the earlier nine put together. Finally, Leslie could stand the tension no longer. "I'm going outside," she whispered to Dad.

The quietness of early morning blanketed the outdoors, incongruous with the struggle being waged for her brother's life. She looked up. Bright streaks of northern lights hovered overhead. The night by the road when she and Dylan discussed the lights leaped into her memory. She could almost feel his arms around her and hear his whisper, "Love can be the music in your midnight." For what must have been the millionth time, she wished for him. First thing when they got home, she'd call him. Just the thought of hearing Dylan's voice brought poignant comfort. She wandered across the wide expanse of lawn, the movement releasing the tension in her muscles. Staring into the sky, she tripped off the curb. She turned to wander back.

Only one other person on the hospital sidewalk shared the pre-dawn gloom. Leslie looked up at the fading streaks in the night sky, then snapped her gaze back to the lone figure striding toward the hospital doors. It couldn't be—She broke into a run, and the figure turned toward her, changed directions, held out his arms.

"Dylan!" She flung herself at him.

He gasped and staggered backward, but tightened his grip around her. "Granny called me. I came as quickly as I could."

"You drove?" Leslie drew back to look into his eyes.

"Not being gifted with wings, that's how I had to do it." He smiled slightly, looking at her as though searching for hidden details. "I couldn't stand the thought of you coping with this all alone. My timing may be lousy, but I've got to know. Will you marry me so we can face whatever happens next together?"

"Yes." She wrapped her arms around his chest, feeling as though she would never let go.

"*What did you say*?" He sounded incredulous.

"I said yes." She laughed at the dawning joy in the green eyes she adored.

"Are you sure? Maybe this isn't the best time—"

She silenced him with a kiss. Slowly his arms tightened around her. He finally pulled away to look at her with love so deep it stopped her breath.

"Thanks for coming," she whispered.

"With a welcome like that, I'll come any time." Twinkles showed through the intense emotion in his eyes.

A light cough indicated they weren't alone. Vince stood

just outside the hospital doors. "Les? Oh, hi, Dylan." He coughed again. "The nurse just came back and said he's going to make it." A tired smile threatened to split his face.

"Thank you, Father." Leslie heard Dylan's fervent whisper. She hugged him joyfully. Tears streamed.

"Honey, look over there." Dylan turned her around, keeping his arms around her.

The northern lights had vanished and a sliver of daylight parted the night sky from the horizon.

A Letter To Our Readers

Dear Reader:

In order that we might better contribute to your reading enjoyment, we would appreciate your taking a few minutes to respond to the following questions. When completed, please return to the following:

Karen Carroll, Editor
Heartsong Presents
P.O. Box 719
Uhrichsville, Ohio 44683

1. Did you enjoy reading *Midnight Music*?
   - ☐ Very much. I would like to see more books by this author!
   - ☐ Moderately

     I would have enjoyed it more if ____________

     ____

2. Are you a member of *Heartsong Presents*? Yes No
   If no, where did you purchase this book? __________

   ____

3. What influenced your decision to purchase this book? (Circle those that apply.)

Cover	Back cover copy
Title	Friends
Publicity	Other ____________

4. On a scale from 1 (poor) to 10 (superior), please rate the following elements.

___Heroine ___Plot

___Hero ___Inspirational theme

___Setting ___Secondary characters

5. What settings would you like to see covered in *Heartsong Presents* books?

____

____

6. What are some inspirational themes you would like to see treated in future books?_______________

____

____

7. Would you be interested in reading other *Heartsong Presents* titles? Yes No

8. Please circle your age range:

Under 18	18-24	25-34
35-45	46-55	Over 55

9. How many hours per week do you read? __________

Name ___________________________________

Occupation ______________________________

Address _________________________________

City ____________ State ______ Zip ________

Heartsong

Great Inspirational Romance at a Great Price!

Heartsong Presents books are inspirational romances in contemporary and historical settings, designed to give you an enjoyable, spirit-lifting reading experience. You can choose from 52 wonderfully written titles from some of today's best authors like Veda Boyd Jones, Linda Herring, Janelle Jamison, and many others.

HEARTSONG PRESENTS TITLES AVAILABLE NOW:

____HP 1 A TORCH FOR TRINITY, *Colleen L. Reece*
____HP 2 WILDFLOWER HARVEST, *Colleen L. Reece*
____HP 3 RESTORE THE JOY, *Sara Mitchell*
____HP 4 REFLECTIONS OF THE HEART, *Sally Laity*
____HP 5 THIS TREMBLING CUP, *Marlene Chase*
____HP 6 THE OTHER SIDE OF SILENCE, *Marlene Chase*
____HP 7 CANDLESHINE, *Colleen L. Reece*
____HP 8 DESERT ROSE, *Colleen L. Reece*
____HP 9 HEARTSTRINGS, *Irene B. Brand*
____HP10 SONG OF LAUGHTER, *Lauraine Snelling*
____HP11 RIVER OF FIRE, *Jacquelyn Cook*
____HP12 COTTONWOOD DREAMS, *Norene Morris*
____HP13 PASSAGE OF THE HEART, *Kjersti Hoff Baez*
____HP14 A MATTER OF CHOICE, *Susannah Hayden*
____HP15 WHISPERS ON THE WIND, *Maryn Langer*
____HP16 SILENCE IN THE SAGE, *Colleen L. Reece*
____HP17 LLAMA LADY, *VeraLee Wiggins*
____HP18 ESCORT HOMEWARD, *Eileen M. Berger*
____HP19 A PLACE TO BELONG, *Janelle Jamison*
____HP20 SHORES OF PROMISE, *Kate Blackwell*
____HP21 GENTLE PERSUASION, *Veda Boyd Jones*
____HP22 INDY GIRL, *Brenda Bancroft*
____HP23 GONE WEST, *Kathleen Karr*
____HP24 WHISPERS IN THE WILDERNESS, *Colleen L. Reece*
____HP25 REBAR, *Mary Carpenter Reid*
____HP26 MOUNTAIN HOUSE, *Mary Louise Colln*
____HP27 BEYOND THE SEARCHING RIVER, *Jacquelyn Cook*
____HP28 DAKOTA DAWN, *Lauraine Snelling*
____HP29 FROM THE HEART, *Sara Mitchell*
____HP30 A LOVE MEANT TO BE, *Brenda Bancroft*

(If ordering from this page, please remember to include it with the order form.)

Presents

____HP31 DREAM SPINNER, *Sally Laity*
____HP32 THE PROMISED LAND, *Kathleen Karr*
____HP33 SWEET SHELTER, *VeraLee Wiggins*
____HP34 UNDER A TEXAS SKY, *Veda Boyd Jones*
____HP35 WHEN COMES THE DAWN, *Brenda Bancroft*
____HP36 THE SURE PROMISE, *JoAnn A. Grote*
____HP37 DRUMS OF SHELOMOH, *Yvonne Lehman*
____HP38 A PLACE TO CALL HOME, *Eileen M. Berger*
____HP39 RAINBOW HARVEST, *Norene Morris*
____HP40 PERFECT LOVE, *Janelle Jamison*
____HP41 FIELDS OF SWEET CONTENT, *Norma Jean Lutz*
____HP42 SEARCH FOR TOMORROW, *Mary Hawkins*
____HP43 VEILED JOY, *Colleen L. Reece*
____HP44 DAKOTA DREAM, *Lauraine Snelling*
____HP45 DESIGN FOR LOVE, *Janet Gortsema*
____HP46 THE GOVERNOR'S DAUGHTER, *Veda Boyd Jones*
____HP47 TENDER JOURNEYS, *Janelle Jamison*
____HP48 SHORES OF DELIVERANCE, *Kate Blackwell*
____HP49 YESTERDAY'S TOMORROWS, *Linda Herring*
____HP50 DANCE IN THE DISTANCE, *Kjersti Hoff Baez*
____HP51 THE UNFOLDING HEART, *JoAnn A. Grote*
____HP52 TAPESTRY OF TAMAR, *Colleen L. Reece*
____HP53 MIDNIGHT MUSIC, *Janelle Burnham*
____HP54 HOME TO HER HEART, *Lena Nelson Dooley*
____HP55 TREASURE OF THE HEART, *JoAnn A. Grote*
____HP56 A LIGHT IN THE WINDOW, *Janelle Jamison*

ABOVE TITLES ARE $2.95 EACH

SEND TO: Heartsong Presents Reader's Service
P.O. Box 719, Uhrichsville, Ohio 44683

Please send me the items checked above. I am enclosing $________
(please add $1.00 to cover postage per order. OH add 6.5% tax. PA and NJ add 6%.). Send check or money order, no cash or C.O.D.s, please.

To place a credit card order, call 1-800-847-8270.

NAME ________________________________

ADDRESS ________________________________

CITY/STATE ____________________ ZIP ________